Passion Never Dies

M. E. Nesser

ISBN: 153499744X
ISBN 13: 9781534997448

for Suzy

Prologue

I was married to the most wonderful man in the world. We had a twenty-seven year romance that was as close to perfect as any couple could ever dream of. I thought I would spend the rest of my life with him. That didn't happen. A year ago, he had a massive heart attack, and he died instantly. Now, at forty-five years old, I am alone. My heart is broken, and I'm finding it impossible to move forward. Being widowed totally and completely sucks.

I'm thankful for our wonderful son, Jackson. He is a reminder of the love I shared with my husband, Bryce, and he has helped me through Bryce's death better than any son should be expected to. But his existence can't fill the incredible void in my heart, and now he's away at college. I feel more alone than ever.

Not everyone can say they experienced true love in their life, but I did. I know I should be grateful for the time we had together, but I want more. I need more. I *deserve* more. Bryce was as constant as the air I breathed, and my longing for him is agonizing.

One night, talking about the future, Bryce and I made a pact: if one of us died, the living spouse promised to find passion in his or her life once more. It sounded like a pretty good plan at the time, but now that it's time to act on that promise, I can't imagine being with another man. The mere thought of it makes that empty feeling even vaster. No other man could love me as much or make me feel as cherished as he did.

We also agreed that, if at all possible, we would send the other person a sign—a reminder that we hadn't completely left. I know it probably sounds silly, but the thought of living without one another was terrifying.

Our agreement provided us with some reassurance that we would never be alone, even if it was just words. The intellectual part of my brain knew at the time that our promise was futile, but now my ability to be logical has been buried with my beautiful husband. I'm a walking zombie in the chaotic world of New York City.

After work, Bryce and I had always taken time to sit down together and talk about our day; it was our chance to catch up on whatever was going on with one another and just to reconnect. Our drink of choice during our special time together was a gin and tonic garnished with two olives. We agreed that if we ever found two pimentos in an olive while drinking a gin and tonic, that would be the sign—and a reminder that we needed to find passion again. In forty-five years, I've never seen two pimentos in any olive, but it seemed like a probable scenario at the time. Now the notion seems absurd.

Time passes quickly. Time drags on. It has been a lifetime since Bryce died—or maybe just a nanosecond. According to the calendar, it has been a year. I am sitting at a quiet bar in Manhattan, having my usual after-work drink and staring into oblivion. I'm feeling void of any emotion; I am exhausted, and barely functioning. I have delegated a staggering amount of my duties to other attorneys in my practice, as well as to the two paralegals I hired to help me deal with my cases. I'm hardly eating or sleeping, and my body is depleted. I know I must look terrible, but I don't care. There is no one to tell me I am beautiful, and I don't think I will ever feel beautiful again. I can't seem to find any beauty around me, either. Living is hard.

I look down at my gin and tonic, trying to find the strength to raise it to my mouth. The bartender gave me two olives, just the way I like it. He has worked here for as long as I can remember. His name is Carl, and he has been married for over twenty years. He can be social, but he can also be quiet and discreet. He knew Bryce, because we came to this bar often, and I can tell he feels sorry for me. He pours my drink without even asking what I want. He engages in conversation only if I initiate it first. Otherwise, he leaves me alone. I'm glad he gives me my space: I don't have the energy for small talk.

This small reminder of our daily ritual should bring me some comfort, but all it brings me is even more despair. I miss Bryce as much today as I did on that fateful day when the police officers came to my office to tell me the news. My eyes cloud with tears, and I know tonight is going to be another long one. I dread going back to our place, but I barely have enough strength left in me to sit up straight at the bar.

I wipe my eyes with the little napkin under my drink and notice something peculiar in my glass. I wipe them again and even shake my head a little, trying to get the exhausted, fuzzy feeling out of my brain. I must be hallucinating—maybe I'm having a psychotic episode. No, this looks real, and I don't think I've become completely crazy quite yet. In front of me is the sign that Bryce and I talked about all those years ago: one of the olives has two pimentos in it. I can barely breathe. Is it possible? Is Bryce sending me a sign? I cover my mouth with my hand so I don't make any strange sounds as the tears stream down my face.

My thoughts race, and my heart is threatening to beat out of my chest. I'm not sure if I'm scared or excited. I pull the olive off the swizzle stick it's perched on and examine it closely, then set it down on a napkin and just stare at it. Too much adrenalin is passing through my body; I feel dizzy. I try to calm myself down, but it's impossible. My hands are shaking, and I'm breathing heavily. Two pimentos? Oh my God, Bryce, what are you trying to tell me?

I'm not sure how long I was sitting there staring at the olive. I was frozen in my seat and finding it difficult to breathe. Suddenly, I had a strange sensation come over me. I could feel someone staring at me. I guess that shouldn't have been surprising, since I was sitting here alone, crying and staring at an olive like it was the most fascinating object in the world. I look up to see a beautiful man with light blue eyes and tussled salt and pepper hair looking my way. He smiles at me, and I can't help but smile back. There's something about him; I can't explain it. Smiling actually feels strange; it has been so long that I've practically forgotten how to bend my mouth that way. Tears still streaming down my face, I look at him quizzically. Who is this man?

"Hi, I'm Ian," he says to me in the deepest, most sultry voice.

I still can't speak. I just stare at him, like I'm having some kind of out-of-body experience. I want to say hello, but the words are trapped inside my head. I look around for other signs of Bryce, but there's nothing. Of course not—he's dead. There's no way he could be at this bar. But now there's this man, and I can't help but stare into his eyes. I open my mouth slightly, more to get oxygen in my lungs than to respond to him.

"Are you OK?" he asks me sympathetically. Oh my God, his voice is intoxicating.

I wipe off my face and try to gather my wits. My hands are shaking. There are two pimentos in my fucking olive. What the hell is happening?

"Do you have a name?" he murmurs, and I wonder if Sirens can appear as men, because this man could definitely lure me with his words.

"It's Katharine," I say in a shaky, barely audible voice.

"Katharine is a beautiful name." He stands up and moves to the empty barstool next to me. I look at him skeptically, but his eyes never leave mine. I feel very confused.

I told this man that my name was Katharine because I made the decision after Bryce died that I would no longer introduce myself as Katie. Bryce always called me Katie, and it was another sad reminder that I couldn't deal with. I had been insisting people call me Katharine since the day he died, and it seems to have stuck.

"Thank you," I reply quietly. I know I must have sounded weak and flustered, but he just kept smiling at me. It was unnerving.

"Can I buy you another drink?" he offers. "You look as though you could use one."

"No thank you. I appreciate the offer, but I don't think I ate anything today, so I better not have another drink or I may fall asleep right here on the bar," I admit.

"You aren't sure if you ate? That means you are most definitely working too hard. It sounds like you need a good meal, Katharine. Please let me buy you dinner."

1

Oh Katie, it worked. I didn't know if it would or not. I've been watching you self-destruct for over a year, and it's breaking my heart. You don't eat. You barely sleep. You rarely smile. Grief is aging you. I never see you hang out with your family or friends anymore. Thank God Jack comes home from Yale once in a while—at least you're forced to have meals with him. And when he's home, you can't sleep on the couch. You sleep in our bed and actually get some rest.

Our bed should bring you wonderful memories, not just sorrowful ones. We made incredible love so often there, and I want you to remember all the passion we shared. I want you to remember how happy our life was. There aren't many people who can say that their love affair started when they were seventeen years old.

We were so lucky to have found each other. We took each other's virginity, and it was the most amazing experience in the entire world. I miss you every day. I don't know why my time was up. There are certain things in our lives that are out of our control. I hate that I was forced to leave, but I am so thankful for every day I had with you. Why can't you embrace my memory—and move on and find some happiness in your life?

It seems to me that you've forgotten the pact we made: neither of us should have to live the rest of our lives alone, remember? That was our deal. You have so much love in your heart, and so much passion in your body. I can't stand by and watch you die while you still have a whole lifetime ahead of you. Don't let my death kill you as well. It isn't fair to our son. Jackson needs you. I need to know that you are OK. Please don't forget how to feel good things. Remember what we promised each other.

Give Ian a chance.

2

inner? I supposed dinner with him would be OK. I was having a hard time thinking clearly, but it was almost as if there
was a little voice in the back of my head urging me to give him
a chance. It should have been unsettling, but for some reason, it wasn't. I
couldn't remember the last time I'd had a full meal. I had definitely not
been to a restaurant for dinner in months. I'd had a few lunch meetings
at restaurants over the past year, but those were strictly business, never
personal. The only dinners I had out at restaurants were with Jackson
when he came home for breaks from school. I guessed a meal with this
man wouldn't hurt. Besides, I definitely needed to eat something.

"Dinner would be nice for a change," I said to him.

"For a change? Most people skip breakfast. Do you make it a habit
to skip dinner?" he asked me with what seemed like genuine concern.

"Not exactly. I um...just work a lot." I wasn't about to explain myself
to this man; I could barely believe I'd said yes to dinner with him. He'd
probably wish I hadn't—the depth of my sadness could fill hours of agonizing conversation. And it would be a conversation that left me even
more heartbroken and desolate. Life was complicated. Actually, life
sucked. Talking about the last year would be excruciating. Why didn't I
eat dinner? Who wanted to eat alone? Also, I just hadn't enjoyed food

since Bryce died. We'd loved to cook gourmet meals and go out to dinner. Eating was another painful reminder of what I'd lost. Besides, my stomach was so knotted up all of the time that it was often hard to swallow water. Coffee was the only form of sustenance that was getting me through my days. Food nauseated me. So yeah, "I work a lot" would suffice for now.

"There's an Italian place a few blocks away. We could walk. Are you game?" he asked me with the most beautiful smile. As he spoke, I swear his eyes sparkled. This masculine Siren was definitely luring me.

"That sounds nice. Thank you," I said. I was feeling timid and unsure, but there was no way I was saying no to him. For some inexplicable reason, I had to go.

He grabbed my hand gently to help me off my barstool. It was a gentlemanly gesture that I found appealing and very sweet. A strange electrical current passed between us when he touched my hand. He must have felt it too, because he looked up quizzically when our skin touched. Time stood still for a moment as we registered the sensation. It was odd, but not frightening. I was about to walk away from the bar when I stopped and looked at the olive.

"Hold on a second. I need to get something," I told him.

I wrapped the olive with the two pimentos in a napkin and slipped it into my purse. I threw a twenty-dollar bill on the bar and said thank you to Carl. I didn't often speak when I was there. I stopped by for a drink almost every day after work and rarely spoke to anyone. Carl gave me the most affectionate smile. I couldn't help but smile back at him. I got the feeling that Carl approved of my leaving with this man. That was reassuring.

Ian gave me a questioning stare when he saw me wrap up the olive, but he didn't say anything. I couldn't imagine what he was thinking, and I really didn't care. There was no way I was leaving that olive on the counter. It was a sign from my beloved husband. I was sure of it. Ian slipped his hand into the crook of my arm and led me out into the street.

The air felt good. After finding the olive and agreeing to dinner, I needed the fresh air, so I was glad he'd suggested we walk instead of hailing a cab. We chatted casually as we walked to the restaurant. He seemed very bright, and our conversation came naturally. It was easy to talk to him. After a few minutes, I could actually feel myself relaxing. I had been in such a fog the past year that I'd forgotten how much I loved this city, especially walking through the streets. There is a life and energy in New York that is constant and liberating. It's hard to explain if you have never been here, but it's wonderful all the same.

Ian made me laugh with his quirky observations about the city. We talked about the staggering price of living in New York. It was obscene how much people paid to live in this crazy place. We noticed a man with a shopping cart resting against a building. He joked that the homeless man had the best rent in town, and it was hard not to laugh with him. Then he handed the man a twenty-dollar bill and thanked him for keeping our streets safe. The man thanked him politely and told us to have a pleasant evening. That, for the first time in far too long, was exactly what I planned to do. Ian took my hand after he handed the man the bill, and we continued to walk toward the restaurant. I thought he might have done it because I looked so frail, but I didn't mind. Holding his hand felt good. He was funny, generous and kind. It was an endearing combination that made me smile.

He teased me about the high-heeled shoes I was wearing, following his ribbing with a compliment on how well I was able to walk in them. He said he couldn't understand how women walked in heels all day. He was convinced that Carrie Bradshaw from *Sex in the City* had put some kind of spell on the women of New York that made them capable of walking for miles in expensive heels. As I looked around, I thought he might be right. There were a lot of women walking up and down the streets in high heels. It cracked me up that not only did he know the name of the show, he knew the main character's name as well. His varied comments and observations were piquing my interest.

When we got to the restaurant, it was really crowded; throngs of people were waiting to be seated. I felt a moment of disappointment that we wouldn't be able to get a table for a long time—I wasn't sure how long I could go without collapsing in exhaustion. He must have sensed my unease, because he grabbed my hand again and walked me past the patrons waiting for tables. As we approached the hostess, she smiled at Ian and said, "Good evening, Mr. Jensen. Two for dinner, sir?"

"Yes please, Andrea."

The hostess grabbed two menus and asked us to follow her into a back seating area that wasn't as loud or as crowded as the main dining area. We sat down, and she handed each of us a menu. She offered Ian a smaller menu—the wine listings, I assumed—with a big smile, and he thanked her graciously.

"You must come here often," I observed.

"Actually, I'm part owner of this place. My brother is my partner. He's also the head chef. I'm so proud of him. It's a great story actually. He's wanted to own a restaurant in New York City since he was a kid. I knew it was only a matter of time before it happened. When he finished his culinary training in Florence, Italy, I offered him the financial backing to open the restaurant. I knew he would make it a huge success. We opened Pane Vino about three years ago, and it has been doing really well since day one," he explained proudly.

"I've heard the food is excellent, but I must admit that I've never eaten here. I haven't really eaten anywhere the past year, though, so that's not saying much. Wow, your brother must put in long hours being the chef. That's tough work. So now that the restaurant has become successful, why doesn't he hire someone to cook for him?"

"He tried hiring other chefs, but they were never consistent. They'd get lazy or take shortcuts, and the food would suffer. The only way to ensure the food is prepared properly is to do it yourself. It *is* a lot of work, but it has been a dream of his for as long as I can remember. He did hire more sous chefs, but he's still here six days a week, sweating away in the kitchen," he explained to me.

I opened up the menu for about two seconds and then closed it again. Making choices wasn't my forte these days.

"Why don't you order for me?" I suggested.

"Is there anything you're allergic to or don't like?" he asked thoughtfully.

"Tripe and liver are the only things I'm not fond of. Other than that, I'll eat just about anything," I assured him.

He ordered several courses, and every morsel was delicious. I don't think I had eaten that much food in the past month in total. It was wonderful, as was the conversation. He sounded like a financial genius. I can honestly say that I've never cared about how much money anyone made. I was always attracted to people's minds and their hearts. But Ian made fiscal strategy sound fascinating. He explained to me that he owned several companies that he kept controlling interest in. He had also made quite a few successful investments.

We spent a great deal of time talking about our children. His eyes lit up when he talked about his daughters. It was endearing when he explained that, after the divorce, they had decided to come live with him. Apparently, his ex-wife didn't really want the responsibility of raising them, but it was still their decision to make. I thought it was interesting that his daughters would prefer to live with their father—it said a great deal about his character. I was fascinated by everything he shared with me; it felt good to think about something other than my grief for once.

At one point, he asked me about what happened at the bar. He prefaced the discussion by saying that I didn't have to share anything with him that was confidential. I appreciated his concern and, for some reason, felt safe enough to tell him what had happened. I told him briefly about my marriage and then about Bryce's untimely death. He seemed genuinely sympathetic about the tradegy that Jackson and I were forced to endure. At that point in the conversation, I wanted to continue. I told him about the pact that I made with my husband. It was comforting that he listened attentively, responded compassionately, and didn't seem surprised when I shared the story about the pimentos. I wasn't exactly sure where this man came from, but I was glad he was introduced into my life.

I thoroughly enjoyed my evening. It was such an unexpected and pleasant surprise. The mixture of wine and food, however, exhausted me. He could tell I was tired, so he called his driver to take me home.

3

Holy cow, Katie, you did it! You finally went on a date. I'm so proud of you. See, it wasn't so bad. This guy is great. He's smart and attractive—and, well, rich. I would hate for some man to use you for any reason and especially take advantage of your financially. He has been divorced for several years, so I'm sure he isn't on the rebound. I love that he has two daughters around Jackson's age. Maybe they can all meet one day and be friends.

It was so good to see you laugh again. I can't stand watching you cry whenever you're alone. And when you're with other people, your mood is always so somber. Your personality has changed so much since I died. I have missed the feisty and vibrant woman that I fell in love with. It seems like such an effort for you to be cheerful. I knew you had it in you to try again. Maybe this is the man who can help you through your sorrow.

I'm also thrilled with how much you ate. You've gotten so thin, and it's such a shame. You're so lovely, and you always had the most beautiful body of any woman I had ever known. I want to see you healthy again! It's so hard not to worry about you.

I love the fact that he acted like such a gentleman. He seemed genuinely sympathetic when you told him about me. The way he held your hand as you told him about how hard this past year has been—it was really sweet. I'm glad he had a driver to take you home. You looked like you were going to collapse by the end of the meal. The way he kissed you on the cheek and thanked you for accompanying him to dinner was so gallant; please see him again! It's time, my love. And remember: I will always love you, my precious Kitten.

4

I don't know what compelled me to ask Katharine to dinner. There was something about how sad and forlorn she looked sitting at the bar all by herself. I felt like I didn't have a choice; I had to talk to her. I hadn't dated in so long, I almost forgot how to ask someone out. It took me several minutes to figure out what to say to her, and the best I could come up with was "Hi, I'm Ian." I shouldn't second-guess myself, though—it worked.

Since my divorce, I hadn't been interested in meeting other women. I lost a lot of faith in women after what my ex-wife did to me. She was cruel and heartless, and I was still reeling from her deceit. But I didn't let it consume me. I focused on my daughters and my businesses and simply put my personal life on hold for awhile. I did have a few one-night stands, but they were never fulfilling. They were just about the sex.

In order to curb what sexual appetite I did have, I spent more time at the gym. It was easier than looking for a relationship. It was a lot less complicated, too. The only problem was that I bulked up quite a bit from all the extra working out and had to have my suits tailored to fit my new physique. I secretly dreamed that someday I would find someone to share the rest of my life with, but I hadn't expected today to be the day.

I can't explain it, but it felt like there was a little voice egging me on and urging me to speak to Katharine. It was incessant, and I'm not sure where it was coming from. I admit that I was watching her from the moment that I sat down at the bar. She seemed so incredibly sad and lonely. There was something that compelled me to talk to her—I wanted to make her smile. I know that New Yorkers like to protect their privacy, but I couldn't stand the despair on this woman's face.

I was watching her and wondering what was making her so sad when I noticed her whole demeanor change as she stared at her glass. It looked like she was drinking a gin and tonic with olives in it—kind of a strange garnish, I thought fleetingly. She picked out one of the olives and stared at it like she had discovered some kind of treasure inside. I couldn't imagine what was so interesting about that olive, but as her eyes filled with tears, I knew I had to say something to her. Everything about the scenario was intriguing.

When I looked into her eyes, I felt a magnetic pull toward her. I wanted to kiss the tears away. I felt like a schoolboy reliving my first crush: I wanted—no, *needed*—to find out more about her. It was obvious she had a story, and I wanted to know what it was. So I did what most guys do when they want to meet a woman: I offered to buy her a drink.

I was disappointed when she turned me down, but I decided to be bold and ask her to dinner instead. I never expected her to accept my invitation, but I was extremely happy that she did. I hadn't had dinner with a woman in months. Katharine looked like she needed a good meal, so I knew I had to take her to Pane Vino, the restaurant I owned with my brother. I knew I could get a table, and I was very proud of my brother's cooking.

As we talked, I was increasingly impressed by Katharine's work ethic and intellect. She was a partner at Stryder, Ross, and Burton, an excellent law firm, and I knew that the kind of law she practiced was difficult and demanding. I had a few friends who worked for the firm and had even used them for a few of the projects I was involved in. I was surprised that our paths had never crossed before this. But I believed in fate—I always had. Maybe I wasn't supposed to meet her until now. There was probably a reason, although what that reason was, I couldn't fathom.

Once she started eating, she became more talkative. Watching her at the bar, I had the impression that she was shy. I couldn't have been more mistaken. She was witty and engaging, and the conversation never lagged throughout the entire meal. At one point, I told her about two of the attorney's I had worked with at her firm. "That sounds a bit chauvinistic. Do you only employ *male* attorney's Ian?" she asked me sternly. "Of course not," I replied nervously. "It was a coincidence that they were both men. I would never discriminate on the basis of a person's gender." I couldn't tell if she was serious or not. She must have sensed my unease and she looked at me straight in the eye and said with the most adorable smirk in her voice, "Since most of the attorney's at our firm are men, I will forgive you this one time." Then we both started laughing.

When she told me about her husband's death the year before, it was hard not to feel her despair. It sounded like she was having a hard time just getting through a day. She had never expected to be widowed at such a young age, and she wasn't dealing with it very well. It explained a lot. She admitted that she never had much of an appetite anymore and that eating alone made her sad. "It's a shame I wasn't overweight when Bryce died, because becoming a widow is a pretty easy way to lose a few pounds. It's a lot less agonizing than counting points at Weight Watchers," she commented with a small smile. Although her comment was sad, I was impressed that she was trying to find a little humor in her predicament. She told me she slept on her couch with her cat because her bedroom had too many memories. I was blown away by her candidness. She was young, bright, and beautiful. She was also wasting away from her grief. I had to do something to help her find joy in her life once again. I couldn't let her follow in her husband's footsteps. There was something incredibly special about this woman, and I needed to be a part of her life.

5

When Ian dropped me off at my building, he got out of the car and escorted me to the door. There was always a security guard at the front entrance, twenty-four hours a day, and Jimmy had been working the night shift for as long as I could remember. He was very saddened when Bryce died; it's hard not to build a rapport with someone you see every day. Jimmy had been very protective of me since my husband passed away. He always asked how I was doing and even asked about my son on a regular basis. He was genuinely fond of Jackson; the two of them loved to talk about basketball and cars. He looked surprised to see me get out of Ian's car that night. He said good evening to us both and gave me the sweetest smile. Maybe I was overthinking it, but I think it was a smile of approval. Ian turned to me, thanked me for accompanying him to dinner, kissed my cheek, and walked back to his car.

Inside the apartment, for the first time since Bryce died, I didn't feel a foreboding presence in the air—everything seemed lighter. I picked up the cat and gave her a hug. She meowed at me, which meant she was hungry. I opened up a can of food and put it in her dish. She ate quickly while I got a glass of water. When she finished, she brushed against my leg and purred. I loved it when she did that. It was very comforting.

I reached down and petted her, and she took off to the couch. She liked to wait for me on the armrest. I walked into the living room and told her that we were going to try the bedroom tonight. She just stared at me. Either she didn't understand me, or she didn't believe it. I called her name several times as I walked into the bedroom to get out of my work clothes. I put on one of Bryce's T-shirts and collapsed into bed. I fell asleep instantly.

It was the first night that I'd slept until morning without interruption since Bryce died. There were no nightmares, and there were no tears. I woke up feeling rested and rejuvenated. It was a new feeling. It felt good. I went into the kitchen, made a cup of coffee, and thought about Ian. He made my heart race like only Bryce had done. It was such a welcoming feeling. Our dinner had been the first pleasurable thing that had happened to me in a very long time. I hoped I would see him again, and the thought made me smile. Then it occurred to me that we had never exchanged numbers. I wanted to thank him for the evening, but I wasn't sure how to contact him. He knew where I worked and lived, so I guess I would have to wait to see if he tried to contact me. Now that I thought about it, though, I wasn't sure I'd ever told him my last name. He'd told me about all of the different things he did for work, but I wasn't sure if he had an actual office or not. I'd never even gotten his last name. The hostess had called him Mister something, but I couldn't remember what. Boy, was I rusty at dating.

I went into the bathroom to shower, pausing to look at myself in the mirror. I looked ridiculously thin. Even my boobs had shrunk. Two or three months ago, I had been forced to buy smaller bras because all of mine had gotten so big on me. I needed to make eating a priority. My dark circles were better today, but my hollow cheeks were horrid. I needed to get my skinny ass to the gym, and I needed to go grocery shopping.

I took a quick shower, grabbed my gym bag and my clothes for work, and headed out the door. Today was a new beginning. I didn't want to die, but if I didn't make some changes, dying could be a distinct possibility. Bryce wouldn't want me to be sad, I told myself. I'd made a promise to him, and I wasn't honoring it. I loved him too much to betray the pact that we'd made to one another. Also, to be honest, I was *tired* of being sad. It took more energy to be depressed than I ever could have imagined. Maybe this Ian man wouldn't be the knight in shining armor who brought me from my depths of despair, but he was definitely a sign. Bryce had sent me a reminder: I truly believed it. It was time I honored the promise I had made to him and started to live again.

6

Until now, I really didn't know if I'd ever be interested in starting another serious relationship. To say that my divorce got pretty ugly at the end would be an understatement, and I didn't want to get hurt like that again. My wife, Monica, became so cold and calculating that it was virtually impossible to remember the fun, loving woman I had married. She became completely self-absorbed, driven by money and possessions; I couldn't get my daughters far enough away from her example. Her goal was to get an obscene amount of money from me so she could live extravagantly and never have to work for the rest of her life.

She started an affair with a personal trainer at the gym at some point during our marriage. I probably will never know for sure when it actually began. It was so humiliating. Our sex life was amazing in the beginning, but then things began to change. The changes were subtle, but they were indications that something was amiss. When I initiated sex she started to push me away, citing headaches, fatigue, and the stress of raising the girls. I knew they were all excuses, but it took awhile for me to catch on. I didn't want to believe she could be unfaithful to me, but her behavior had changed so drastically: it occurred to me that if she didn't want to have sex with me, she was likely having it with someone else. I was so lonely the last couple years of our marriage. She even lost any interest in spending time with our girls. It got to the point where our nanny was doing all of the caring for them.

It wasn't until I hired a private detective that I learned of her infidelity. It broke my heart. I loved my wife. She was the mother of our beautiful daughters. I loved the family we had made. What the hell had happened? My wife had turned into someone I didn't even recognize, selfish and greedy. My girls didn't want anything to do with her either. It was so sad. I gave her a decent settlement and ended the marriage with as much dignity as I could muster. Last I heard, she was living in a high-rise apartment with her personal trainer.

Now Katharine had come into my life, and I couldn't wait to see her again. But I realized last night, lying in bed thinking about all of the things we'd talked about, that I'd never gotten her cell number. Heck, I didn't even know her last name. Fortunately, I knew where she worked. I could barely sleep trying to figure out the best way to contact her again.

I didn't want to scare her, but I had to see her again. Our dinner was one of the best nights I'd had in years. Every woman I had gone out with since my divorce had left me feeling empty and discouraged. There was a part of me that had given up on the notion of falling in love again. Katharine was different. She challenged my intellect in ways I never thought I'd experience again—and she was beautiful.

Love? What was I thinking? I'd spent three hours with this woman, and my mind was already reeling with emotion. It was crazy. Now I had to decide how to proceed. First, I needed to send her a thank-you. Yes, that was what I needed to do. When we were doing the twenty-questions thing last night, I had asked her what her favorite color was. She'd said it was yellow, because it reminded her of sunshine. It was fitting. I could see hints of a sunny personality dying to emerge from her saddened state. That's when I got the idea.

I called the florist I used for my businesses and asked her to put a variety of yellow flowers together. Roses seemed too serious after one meal, and since I didn't know what her favorite flower was, I asked for an assortment. The florist said I needed an accent color to make the arrangement prettier, so I suggested purple. When we were talking about our favorite colors, I'd told Katharine that I was always drawn toward the color purple because it was fun and daring. I hoped the purple accents would make Katharine think of me. I decided to send the bouquet to her office; her home might have been too personal.

The next big decision was what to write on the card. I scribbled a variety of different sentiments on a notepad. Some were corny. Others were too long. It was a lot harder than I thought it would be. I felt like a silly teenager all over again. I ended up writing, "Thank you for last night. I hope to see you again—Ian."

I went to the firm's website and found Katharine's last name, and I asked the florist to deliver the flowers as soon as possible. She said they would be delivered between two and four in the afternoon. I was pleased with my decision. It was strange, but not only did I want to see Katharine again, I felt like I *had* to. Now I had to wait and see what her next move was going to be.

7

I showed up at work with a renewed sense of energy. As soon as I took off my coat and put my briefcase away, I asked my staff to join me in the conference room. They glanced at one another, nervous about the impromptu meeting. I hoped their trepidation would be quelled when they realized my intent. In fact, I was confident they would be very pleased by my sudden change of heart. The atmosphere had been very sullen in our offices; it was time for a serious change. I regretted making my dedicated personnel suffer due to my personal loss. I hadn't shown any enthusiasm at work since Bryce died, and they had learned to tiptoe around me and keep our exchanges succinct. It was time to rally my crew back into normalcy.

I started out by thanking them all for stepping up the past year through my excruciating mourning period. They looked at me sadly. I told them that I was ready for a fresh start, and their faces lightened up. I could feel the vibe getting happier in the room as the meeting progressed. We discussed our ongoing cases and a few prospective new ones. I had an excellent staff. They were hardworking and bright, and it was time to reward them with kickass legal work. I offered them new incentives and bonus opportunities, and I could feel their renewed excitement. Today was a brand-new day.

When I adjourned the meeting, my staff returned to their desks with smiles and laughter. It occurred to me that the entire staff had shared in my somber existence. Not anymore. There was a part of me that felt terribly guilty about letting things get so dismal. But there was nothing I could do about it now except change the way things were run and make it better. It was time to get back to doing what we all loved. The law was waiting for us to grab it by the reins and find success again.

The morning flew by. I had a lot of work to catch up on. I needed to reacquaint myself with the cases that we were working on. It was time to stop expecting my paralegals to do all of the work for me. At 11:30 a.m. I sat back to take a sip of water and felt something strange—I was hungry. It had been a long time since I'd had that sensation. I knew that I owed my staff for all of their hard work and loyalty, so I called a local deli and had a smorgasbord of food sent to the conference room. The staff was shocked when the delivery arrived. Everyone congregated in the conference room and had a hearty lunch, including me. Morale had escalated, and I was satisfied—for now. I owed these people so much more than this, but it was a start.

The afternoon passed as quickly as the morning had; I hadn't realized how behind I had gotten. At 3:30 p.m. my secretary knocked on my door and said I had received a delivery. I couldn't imagine what it could have been—I hadn't ordered anything in ages. I told her to bring it in. When she walked in with a huge bouquet of yellow and purple flowers, I felt such warmth. When was the last time someone had sent me flowers? Oh yeah, when Bryce died. But now was not the time to dwell on that. I asked her who they were from, and she said there was a card, but it was in a sealed envelope with my name on it.

She set the flowers on my desk, smiled at me, and scurried out of the office, closing the door behind her. I opened up the card. Holy cow, it was from Ian. He'd enjoyed himself as much as I had. This was such a sweet gesture. I didn't know men could still be gallant in this day and age. The arrangement was stunning. I had never seen such a variety of yellow flowers in my life. And the choice of accent colors didn't escape me. When he'd said he liked purple because it was fun and daring, I'd been intrigued. Now I had a problem, though. I wanted to thank him for the flowers, but I still didn't have a contact number for him.

Then I got an idea. I called the restaurant and asked to speak with Todd. Ian had introduced me to his brother the night before, so he knew who I was. I apologized for bothering him, but I told him I wanted to thank his brother for a lovely evening and didn't have his phone number. He gave it to me freely.

"Thank you for bringing some light into my brother's life," Todd told me. "I haven't seen him smile like that in a very long time."

"It was your brother who turned the light on for me, Todd," I admitted. "I'd been living in darkness for way too long."

"Then it sounds like a match made in heaven. Ian is a really good man. He was totally screwed by that bitch wife of his. He deserves so much better. Good luck, Katharine. I wish you both the best."

We hung up, and I sat there, stunned. I was good for Ian? That was not what I expected to hear. I'd been feeling so pathetic that it had never occurred to me that I could be beneficial in someone else's life. Todd's comment made me feel really good. Our short, but poignant, conversation gave me just the right amount of confidence to respond to Ian with a renewed sense of enthusiasm.

8

$\mathcal{G}$ was getting very little done at work, so I decided to go to the gym. I worked out with my personal trainer and then ran for close to an hour on the treadmill. I couldn't concentrate. I waited impatiently to hear something from Katharine. Around four o'clock, I called the florist to see if the flowers had been delivered. They had been. I felt like a teenager waiting to see if the girl I'd asked to the prom would say yes or not. It was such a strange feeling. I hoped she didn't think the flowers were a premature gesture, but I had to do something. Last night had meant a lot to me.

As I was leaving the gym, my phone rang. I didn't recognize the number.

"Ian Jensen," I answered.

"Hi, Ian. It's Katharine," she said.

"Katharine, hello. What a pleasure to hear from you!" I said, maybe a bit over enthusiastically.

"I wanted to thank you for the flowers. They're so beautiful. You didn't have to do that," she said in the most soothing voice.

"You're so welcome. Beautiful flowers for a beautiful lady." I instantly felt embarrassed by my corny reply.

"Thank you. That's the nicest thing I've heard in a long time."

"I'm only into honesty and facts, Katharine. And the fact is that last night was really special for me. I was hoping—would you be interested in going out with me again sometime?" I asked nervously.

"I'd love to," she said without hesitation.

"Are you free tonight? I know you need to work on that not skipping dinner thing, and there's no reason either of us should eat alone. Besides, I don't want to go another day without seeing you," I admitted. Yep, I sounded like a lovesick, pathetic schoolboy, and I didn't care.

"You know what? I did make the conscious decision to work on that eating thing, and I really don't like eating alone. I'd love to see you again as well. I was sorry to see last night end."

We arranged to meet at the entrance of her office building after work. There was a quaint French bistro near her office that I knew had excellent food. I was a friend of the owner, so I knew I'd be able to get a table. I called him as soon as I hung up from speaking with Katharine. Jacques was thrilled that I had a date. He was the kind of Frenchman who believed in good food, good wine, and frequent lovemaking with a good woman. He was a true romantic who gave me a hard time about not looking for love after the divorce. The restaurant was small and intimate. It would give us the chance to talk in a less boisterous environment, giving us a chance to know each other better. That was my goal. I needed to know everything there was to know about this woman.

9

oly crap, what was happening? I had just agreed to a second date with a man I'd just met. I couldn't believe how excited I was. I walked into the private bath located next to my office and looked at myself in the mirror. I was dressed in a severely tailored pinstriped suit, and I had put my hair up in a twist like I did every morning. Shit, I really looked like an attorney. This wouldn't do. I needed to do something to spruce myself up. I hadn't been on a date in nearly thirty years, and while it was exciting, it was also nerve wracking. My palms were sweaty, so I washed them. I even splashed some cold water on my face. Was I really doing this?

I walked back out to the reception area and asked to speak with my secretary Suzie in private. She walked into my office and closed the door quietly behind her.

"Is everything OK?" she asked me with a genuinely worried expression on her face.

"I need a favor," I said anxiously.

"Sure, what's up?" Suzie asked me.

"Um, I, um have a dinner date tonight—" I began.

"I knew it! I told the gang that you must have met someone. That's so awesome, Katharine. What do you need me for? Ask me anything—I'm all yours," she said enthusiastically.

"He's picking me up here after work, and I look like such a lawyer," I said futilely.

"Give me a second," she said and ran out of the room.

Suzie came back with a big orange bag. She motioned for me to sit down in one of the chairs I use for my clients and stared at my face intently.

"What are you doing?" I asked her.

"You're looking better, but you're still too thin. And you have dark circles. I need to do something with this face. Just give me a minute. I went to beauty school before I got my business administration degree. I have all sorts of tricks in this bag," she said with a wicked gleam in her eye.

For the next twenty minutes, she applied lights layers of makeup to my face. I felt young and giddy. It was fun to do this. No one had put makeup on my face since my wedding. It was more relaxing than I remembered. I had hardly seen any of my girlfriends over the past year, so this was a nice change of pace. It was neat to hang out with another woman and talk about girl stuff. I just sat there and let her play with her makeup. I'm not sure who was more excited. It was obvious that she was very good at this and enjoyed it thoroughly. Although I loved having her as a secretary, I wondered why she hadn't gone into a career in the beauty industry. It was obvious that she was very passionate about it.

When she seemed satisfied with my makeup, she started to take the pins out of my hair and started brushing it. That felt so good. I closed my eyes and just enjoyed how it felt. No one had touched me in so long that I'd forgotten how much I craved it. Bryce used to brush my hair and massage my scalp. It was such a great sensation. She pulled out the rest of the pins and did something with the front of my hair so it didn't fall haphazardly in my face, then she told me to close my eyes while she teased and sprayed my hair.

"Voila! You're gorgeous!" she exclaimed.

I got up and went into the bathroom to check out what she had done to me. I didn't recognize the woman in the mirror. My eyes filled with tears. Suzie ran in to see if I liked it.

"You can't cry! It'll ruin all of my hard work!" she yelled at me.

"I'm so sorry. I haven't seen this Katharine in way too long," I admitted.

"Well, it's about time," she scolded me.

"Yeah, I think you're right. I can't thank you enough, Suzie," I said. I was so overwhelmed with emotion that I did something very out of character: I hugged her.

"Any time. And can I make one more suggestion? You should think about undoing those top two buttons on your blouse. You look like a nun like that." We both laughed at her remark. Sadly, I had been living like a nun for over a year. The prospect of not living in chastity was terrifying as well, but I'd deal with that hurdle when I came to it. First things first.

With that remark, she turned and left my bathroom. I stared at myself for a long time. The girl had some talent—I actually looked pretty. I hadn't felt like this in ages. It was a really good feeling. "I think I am ready for this," I thought to myself. I did as she'd suggested and unbuttoned my top two buttons to reveal a little cleavage. Suzie was right; unbuttoning my blouse made me look sexier. I put on some more deodorant and a little perfume and brushed my teeth. After reapplying more lipstick, I had to sit down. This was overwhelming, and I needed a minute to compose myself before I went downstairs. If nothing else, at least I knew I looked a lot better than I had yesterday.

10

I got to the entrance of her building about fifteen minutes before we were supposed to meet. I had met with presidents and secretaries of state, and I'd never been as nervous as I was right now. This could be a pivotal point in my life. For the first time in years, I think I was ready to be in a relationship again. It thrilled me. It also scared the living shit out of me.

I entered her building five minutes before our scheduled time and paced the foyer. Every time I heard the elevators open, I stared at them in anticipation. I had been on dozens of dates since my divorce, and I'd never felt like this. I think I actually had butterflies in my stomach. My palms were even a little sweaty, which was a new sensation as well. I was really excited to see her again. God, I hoped she felt the same way about seeing me.

When Katharine finally exited the elevator, I felt like a tidal wave had struck me. She was stunning! I'd thought she was beautiful when we met the night before, but the woman walking toward me now was breathtaking. I smiled at her, and she blushed. She walked confidently toward me and extended her hand to take mine. I leaned forward and kissed her cheek. She smelled divine. I let the kiss linger and whispered in her ear, "You look absolutely breathtaking."

She leaned her head back, looked me in the eyes, and said with the most beautiful smile, "You look pretty breathtaking yourself, Mr. Jensen."

There was no way I was letting go of her hand, so I held on tight and escorted her out of the building. We chatted the whole way to the restaurant, never letting go of each other's hands. She was carrying a briefcase, so as soon as we were outside, I took it from her hand and carried it for her.

She had never been to the bistro before and was excited to be going there. Jacques approached us as we entered the restaurant, gushing about my beautiful date. It was actually a little embarrassing. He took Katharine's arm from me and escorted her to the table, chatting with her the whole way. I followed like a puppy dog. After he seated us, he patted me on the back and said, "It's about time, my dear friend." Then he quietly disappeared. Before we had a chance to order anything, sparkling water and a fabulous bottle of French wine were brought to the table, compliments of the owner.

It was a small, intimate restaurant with soft, French music in the background. Since Katharine was new to this restaurant, she let me do the ordering. I loved being able to do that for her: I knew what it felt like to make decisions all day at work, and it was refreshing to have someone else take on the responsibility now and again. Whenever I'd ordered for my ex, she would find something to complain about. Even if she loved what I picked out for her, she bitched about something. Sharing a meal with Katharine was turning out to be so much more pleasant, and it was only our second dinner together. Katharine also loved drinking wine as much as I did, and Jacques had picked a fabulous vintage. As soon as our glasses were poured, I toasted to eating dinner with a special woman two nights in a row. Even though we barely knew each other, I knew she was special. She smiled, thanked me, and took a sip.

I'd never been able to sit and talk with a woman as easily as I did with Katharine. At one point during the meal, she asked about my marriage. "Last night I spilled my heart to you about my husband, would you care to share what happened with your wife?" she asked me cautiously. "Of course. Let's see...where to begin?" I thought for a minute before I responded. "Monica was so much fun when we met. She was full of life and we had such a blast together. We met our senior year in college. When we graduated from college, it seemed like the natural progression to get married. She said she wanted children, but now I'm not so sure. After our first daughter Emily was born, Monica got really depressed. She had a really hard time caring for her. Thankfully, our mothers' were able to take turns watching the baby. Before we knew it, she was pregnant again. At this point in my career I was finding a lot of success and making a decent living. After our second daughter Sara was born, she asked for a nanny...then a housekeeper. Before I knew it, she wasn't spending any time with our girls. She became very demanding. She wanted a breast augmentation and a tummy tuck. She was charging obscene amounts of money on our credit cards. She spent a lot of time away from home. I didn't know where she was going or what she was doing. It got to the point where we were no longer intimate and we barely spoke to one another. I knew something was going on. Finally, I hired a private detective to follow her. It didn't take him long to figure out what was going on. She was having an affair with a guy at the gym. I was devastated. I knew I couldn't stay with a woman who was unfaithful, so I told her she needed to get out. She was happy to leave as long as I gave her a ton of money and agreed to keep the kids. I shouldn't have been surprised that she didn't want the children, but I was. So we got a divorce, and I got full custody of our girls. Not a fairytale romance, huh?"

"Oh, Ian, I am so sorry," Katharine said as she took my hand lovingly. "I am so sorry for you and your daughters. I cannot imagine how any woman could give up custody of her children."

"It has been really difficult on the girls," I told her sadly.

"Of course. It has to be hard on all of you. They are lucky to have you, though. And I have to wonder why any woman in her right mind would cheat on you?" she said with a smile.

"Well, thank you for that compliment, Mrs. Collins. To be honest, I don't think I'll ever understand why anyone has the need to be unfaithful. I believed in the vows we took, and I thought Monica and I would be married forever. Getting a divorce never entered my conscious mind. When I learned of her betrayal, I felt like I had been stabbed in the heart. The pain was inmeasurable. I loved her so much and I gave her everything she wanted, but it still wasn't enough."

Before I knew it, over two hours had passed, and our dinner had ended. I didn't want the evening to be over, but I didn't want to pressure her into anything; I knew it was too soon. My attraction to her was growing by the minute. She was intoxicating, and I wanted to suck up every ounce of her presence.

"Would you like to leave?" I asked her reluctantly.

"Not really," she said honestly.

"Neither would I. Why don't we walk toward your place, and if you get tired, we could always call my driver and ask him to pick us up?"

"That sounds like a great idea. I've eaten more in the past two days than I've eaten in the last year," she said with a laugh.

"Then a walk will do us both some good," I said. Jacques rushed over to kiss us good-bye. We thanked him for the wine and the magnificent food. He thanked Katharine for forcing my stubborn American heart to open up to possibilities again. It probably sounded like a strange comment to her, but I knew exactly what he meant. And he was right. She had forced me to believe I might have a chance to find love again. I think she understood as well and blushed at the compliment. I stood up and took her hand, and we left the bistro. It was a beautiful night, and I was thrilled that she'd agreed to the walk home. I needed to savor every minute with her. She was as exquisite as the bottle of wine we'd had with dinner. "It's always disappointing when the bottle is empty," I thought, "but the good news is that, if you play your cards right, there is usually another bottle that can be consumed on another day—and it will be just as enjoyable."

11

I'd never thought I would feel this comfortable with another man again. Ian was incredible. He was smart, funny, and extremely charismatic. Moreover, he was incredibly sexy. That was something new to me, feeling turned on by another man. Every part of my body felt alive near him. I was mesmerized every time I looked into his bright blue eyes. He was taller than Bryce, with a more muscular physique, which I found quite appealing. But it was his deep, masculine voice, like sex and poetry intertwined, that really did me in. He probably could have brought me pleasure with his voice alone. Actually, he already did.

Ian stirred feelings in me that I thought had died. My head was conflicted by my attraction to Ian, but my body and heart were enamored with him. It was all happening so quickly. I was excited. I was scared. I wanted to touch him. More importantly, I wanted him to touch me back. It looked like I might be finding passion again.

Dinner was delicious, and Jacques was a riot. He was definitely a consummate romantic, and it was obvious that he was excited about our being there together. I didn't want the evening to end, but I was exhausted from a long day at work, my first visit to the gym in months, and the rich food we had just eaten. Walking home was a great idea. It would keep me awake and give me more time with him.

Conversation with him was so easy. We had so much to talk about. I'd spoken more over the past two evenings than I had in the year since my husband died. It was nice, but it was also tiring. Was I really that run down? I suppose I was. As we approached my apartment building, I started to get nervous. Did he expect to come in? I wasn't sure I was ready to sleep with him yet; in fact, I knew I wasn't. Everything was happening way too fast. I didn't want the night to end, but I was really tired. Oh crap, what was I going to do? I didn't want to reject him or hurt his feelings. I hadn't dated in so long that I wasn't sure what was expected.

Jimmy was standing outside the building. He smiled at me genuinely and said good evening to the both of us. He opened the door, and we walked into the foyer. Ian must have sensed my unease, because he handed me my briefcase.

"Once again, thank you so much for such a lovely evening, Katharine," he said to me.

"Thank you, Ian," I gushed, relieved. "Thank you for everything. You could not have come at a more important time in my life. I felt like I was dying. Who am I kidding? I *was* dying. You reminded me that I have something to live for. To be honest, being with you made me realize that I don't have to die yet, and I can't thank you enough for that..." I trailed off, looking down at the ground.

He gently lifted my chin, so I was forced to gaze into his eyes. "You are young and beautiful, and you have a long life in front of you. I'm so glad I walked into that bar last night," He continued to hold my chin and gently rubbed his thumb over my mouth. I closed my eyes and enjoyed the sensuous gesture. When I opened my eyes, he was staring at me.

"So am I," I said as tears started to pool in my eyes.

Ian leaned in close and kissed me, gentle and sweet. I kissed him back. It felt wonderful, but it didn't last long enough. I was confused. I wanted more, but I knew I wasn't ready. So did he. After the kiss ended, he looked me in the eyes. I could tell he was trying to figure out how I'd felt about the kiss. I smiled up at him, giving him my answer. He smiled back, and I could feel myself blushing. Experiencing a first kiss as an adult was really strange.

"Thank you for a wonderful evening, Katharine. I hope you sleep well," he said. With that said, he turned away from me for a second night in a row and walked out of my building. I stood there frozen until I saw his car pull in front of my building to collect him and he drove away.

I went upstairs, fed the cat, and collapsed on my bed. There was a part of me that had really wanted to invite him up to my place, but there was a bigger part of me that was too scared. I was grateful that he was a gentleman, but his departure had left me with an empty feeling; it was disconcerting. A lot had happened in the past twenty-four hours, and I was conflicted. Ian was amazing. I wanted him to make love to me more than I'd wanted anything for a very long time. Oh my God, I wanted him to make love to me. I couldn't believe it. Was I finally ready to move on?

12

$\mathcal{L}$eaving Katharine was one of the hardest things I'd done in a long time. Part of me wanted to touch her everywhere and never let her go, but another part of me understood that I couldn't rush her. She'd been so sad when I met her. Even though it was obvious that meeting me had lifted her spirits, I didn't think she was ready for more quite yet. I planned to take this as cautiously as need be—I didn't want to screw this up. I couldn't believe how much I wanted this relationship to work. God, the kiss had felt so good to me. It was crazy how fast I was falling for this woman.

I called her the next morning and thanked her again for dinner. She sounded excited to hear from me, and we talked for about twenty minutes. I wanted to see her again badly, but I didn't want to overwhelm her. All night I had been brainstorming about something we could possibly do together over the weekend. I was excited when I came up with an idea. I asked her if she'd be interested in going hiking on Saturday.

"Hiking?" she asked in a surprised voice. "Where could you possibly hike in New York?"

"Yeah, hiking. You know, that crazy activity where you walk around outside and enjoy nature. I love the outdoors. I love the city, but I need to get out of it from time to time. There's a great place to hike about an hour away, Anthony's Nose Hike. It overlooks Bear Mountain. I love going there in the morning. It takes about two hours to do the hike, and I was hoping you'd want to go with me."

"That sounds amazing. I haven't done anything outdoorsy for the longest time. In fact, unless the streets of New York count, I can't remember doing anything outside. That's a great idea—the fresh air would probably do me some good."

"Oh, I'm so glad. Then it's a date. Would it be OK to pick you up around nine in the morning?"

"That's sounds perfect. I'll be ready."

"Did you have anything planned on Saturday, or can you spend the whole day with me?"

"I don't have any plans. Thank you again so much for asking."

"That's great! See you Saturday!"

13

I was excited about Saturday. I hadn't done anything fun on the weekend in over a year. I had been invited to dinners and such, but I'd politely declined every invitation; getting dressed up and making idle conversation sounded like a nightmare to me. It was so good to be looking forward to an activity that didn't include being alone and being sad. The prospect of doing something different—actually, doing something at all—gave me a renewed sense of energy and life.

I did have a big problem, though. I didn't have hiking boots. I asked my secretary to find me a place to buy some shoes after work, and she found one two blocks from our office. You have to love the city—it has everything available at your disposal. As soon as I finished my day, I hustled to the shoe store and bought some black hiking boots. They weren't as scary as I'd expected. In fact, they were kind of cute, and I knew they'd look even better with jeans instead of my pencil skirt. There was something empowering about bulky, black boots: I felt like a badass in them. I was used to wearing expensive heels, and these boots made me feel different—exactly what the doctor ordered.

I picked up some sushi and went home to start packing. Since Ian wanted me to spend the day with him on Saturday, I figured that I should have a change of clothes for lunch and possibly dinner. I should have asked him more questions. Where would we have lunch, and were we going to be together through the dinner hour as well? I assumed that we would, so I put together a few outfits so I would be prepared for anything.

I poured a glass of wine and sat in front of the fire eating my sushi, Tabby curled up next to me. I listened to Anita Baker and stared at the flames, feeling happy for the first time in ages. It was a foreign feeling for me, and it felt good for a change. I was so excited about Saturday. I hadn't looked forward to doing anything in the longest time. I wanted to spend the day with Ian. I wanted to get to know him better. What I really wanted to do was kiss him again. He had been teasing me with that gentle kiss, and I was craving so much more.

Since I felt better, I thought I would give Jack a call. I hadn't heard from him all week. No matter how busy he was, he always picked up the phone when I called him. It was just the two of us now, and he was very protective of me. It was so sweet. He answered on the second ring. I was asking him about his classes when he interrupted me and said that I sounded different. I told him that I had gone out with a friend for dinner the night before and was starting to feel better. He seemed genuinely pleased with that information and congratulated me for going out into the big, bad world. I even told him that I planned to go hiking on Saturday and had even purchased a pair of hiking boots. That made him laugh; he found it hard to believe I was going to do any kind of physical activity, especially outdoors. The news surprised him so much that he never asked who I was going with. I was glad for that. I didn't know what was happening with Ian, and I wasn't ready to try to put it into words yet. Over the past year, Jackson had had to be the adult in our relationship. We chatted for about twenty minutes, and then he said he was off to meet some friends. I was glad I'd called him. I wanted Jack to know I was feeling better, he worried so much. I hoped that my call had brought him some peace.

I brought Tabby to bed with me and tried to read. I couldn't concentrate. All I could think of was Ian. It had only been one day since I'd seen him, and I found myself missing him. I did not want to wait until

Saturday to talk to him again. I wondered if he was thinking of me. Oh, what the hell. I decided to give him a call.

He answered on the first ring.

"Katharine, what a nice surprise. Have a good day?" he said in the sexiest voice I had ever heard.

"I did. I was having a hard time falling asleep. I hope you don't mind that I called this late. I wanted to tell you that I'm looking forward to Saturday," I admitted to him sheepishly.

"I wish tomorrow was Saturday," he said dreamily. Wow, I hadn't expected him to say that. It was an incredible feeling knowing this man was looking forward to being with me.

"Me too. Do you have plans tomorrow night?" I asked him boldly.

"Actually, I have a charity dinner tomorrow night. It's a fundraiser for breast cancer. My mom is a survivor. She had both breasts removed when she was fifty-three. It was stage three, and pretty aggressive—it's a miracle she's still with us. I'm part of the team that organizes the event. Hey, I have an idea. How would you like to come with me?"

"Oh, no. That isn't necessary. I'd hate to intrude on your night. I was just asking. Have a great time with your mother tomorrow. I can wait until Saturday," I said, trying to hide the disappointment in my voice.

"Are you kidding? My mom would be thrilled if I brought someone with me for once. I've been going to these things solo for years. We call it the B52 Ball, since she was fifty-two when she was diagnosed. It would be great to have you there with me." The way he said it made me believe him.

"If you're sure? I'm actually a little embarrassed for being so forward," I said reluctantly. "Sometimes that forward, attorney-side of my personality rears it's little head. Hopefully, it isn't a trait you find unpleasant."

"On the contrary. I love a self-assured and direct woman. As for tomorrow evening, nothing would please me more than to have you by my side. It's a black tie event, so you'll need to dress up. Do you have something to wear?"

"I'm sure I can figure something out. What time should I be ready?" I asked him excitedly.

"I'll pick you up at seven. The event starts at eight, but I need to get there early and make sure everything is ready when the doors open. I know you work all day. Is that too early for you? I could always have my driver pick you up after he drops me off."

"I'll be ready. I'd be more comfortable arriving with you. Besides, I usually kick the staff out promptly at five on Fridays, no matter what. They tend to work late throughout the week, so I insist that everyone leave at a decent hour when the week is over. I'll cab it home instead of walk—that will give me plenty of time to get ready."

14

I had thought about asking Katharine to the event, but I didn't want to overwhelm her or be too presumptuous. I didn't know if asking her to a black tie event that was so personal to me would be too much this soon in our relationship. I hadn't dated anyone seriously since my divorce, so the only female companions I'd brought to the B52 Ball in the last few years were my daughters. On one hand, it seemed early in our relationship to subject her to my mom. On the other hand, I didn't want to go another day without seeing her. Not seeing her on Thursday had been hard enough. I'd thought about calling her all day, but I didn't want her to think I was being pushy. I couldn't believe how relieved I was when she called me last night. I felt like a love-sick teen-ager, and it was a pleasant feeling for a change.

The next day dragged by so slowly; I couldn't even count the number of times I looked at the clock. I was excited to show Katharine off as my date. She was beautiful, smart, and sophisticated, and I knew I'd feel proud having her by my side. I left the office early, because I wasn't getting much accomplished. I went to the gym and worked out hard for over an hour, hoping exercise would curb the sexual energy that was growing inside of me. It didn't help. I knew I had to take it slow with Katharine, but I didn't want to. I couldn't believe how ready I was to move forward with this relationship. I didn't think I had ever desired a woman this much. I would wait for her cues before I tried anything, but I couldn't help kissing her the other night. The way she looked at me drew me in like a siren. I felt like an idiot running from her so quickly after the kiss, but I had to get away from her before I did something premature that we both might regret.

I arrived at her apartment building about fifteen minutes early. It was a habit of mine to arrive early for appointments; I never wanted anyone to have to wait for me. Being punctual was important in my business, so I made it a priority in my personal life to be early as well. I walked up to the front entrance, and the doorman called up to Katharine's unit. He gave me a sincere smile and even addressed me by my surname. She messaged that she was on her way down, and I felt giddy with anticipation.

When she stepped out of the elevator, I couldn't believe how stunning she looked. She wore a form-fitting black dress that plunged low at the neckline, accentuating the most beautiful breasts I had ever seen. How had I not noticed those before? The dress gathered at her waist, making it look petite and delicate, and her hips flared out just enough that I could picture myself hanging on to them as I made love to her. Her hair had been curled and was up in a loose twist that made me want to suck on her neck. She was utter perfection. I was completely mesmerized. Katharine Collins was a vision to behold, and I could feel stirrings in my body just at the sight of her. This could potentially be a very long evening, because I was already getting hard.

Her physicality wasn't the only thing attracting me to her, however. Her outward beauty only added to my growing fascination. What I was feeling went way beyond sexual attraction. I felt an overwhelming desire to protect this woman. I wanted to make her laugh. I needed to make her feel love again. I wanted to take her dancing. I wanted to sit by a fire sipping wine and share intimate thoughts with her. Was love at first sight really a thing? It must be, because it had to be love I was experiencing. I just stood there looking at her, saying nothing. I wanted to freeze-frame this moment.

"You're staring, Ian. Is everything OK?" she asked me with the most adorable smirk.

"I can't help it. You are probably the most beautiful woman I have ever seen," I told her honestly. With that admission, her cheeks flushed. The added radiance in her face made her even more angelic. I was doomed. Where had this woman been all of my life?

"Why thank you. It feels good to get dressed up in something other than a suit. And thank you again for letting me tag along. I still feel guilty about being so forward; I don't know the standard protocol for asking a man out these days. I'm glad I said something, though. I've been looking forward to the evening all day!"

"Me too," was the extent of my reply. I was still paralyzed by her magnificence.

15

*I*an looked so scrumptious in his tuxedo that I felt flustered when I first saw him. His suit must have been tailored to his incredible physique, and the way he was staring at me was lethal. It felt like he was going to pounce at any moment—and, God, how I wanted him to do just that.

Ian's staring told me that he thought I looked good, too. I'd had my hair and makeup done on the way home and then taken a bath to wash my body off. I was wearing one of my favorite Armani dresses; I'd been worried that it would be too big since I was down about ten pounds, but it was actually more comfortable a little looser. It was too warm for nylons and I hated panty lines, so I decided to forego underwear all together. It felt a bit provocative of me, but that added to the excitement of the evening. Even if the date never progressed to that level, being bare under my dress was thrilling. It felt like my naughty little secret that I hoped to share with him one day. Most importantly, I'd wanted to look elegant. Now, eyes locked with Ian's, I felt confident that I had succeeded. He looked like he wanted to consume me. It was an incredibly exciting feeling. It was raw and oh, so hot.

He took my hand and walked me to his car—tonight he had picked me up in a stretch limousine. The driver opened the door for us and gently closed the door once we were situated. We sat across from each other. It felt strange at first, but it made for easier conversation. Ian offered me a glass of champagne, which I gladly accepted. It was a bottle of Krug: he was going all out tonight. Krug was the caviar of champagnes, but it was also my favorite. I wondered how he knew that.

"Are you trying to woo me with expensive champagne, Mr. Jensen?" I teased him.

"Is it working?" he asked me in that seductive voice that just about sent me over the edge.

"I'll reserve judgment until later, but I'm flattered by the niceties thus far."

Sipping our champagne, we talked casually about the day. Our conversation flowed freely, but I couldn't help assessing everything about him. He had slicked his hair back, which made him look even more handsome and distinguished. He had pronounced facial features, stoic and very masculine, and set off by dimples as adorable as I had ever seen. And his blue eyes made me swoon. He had beautiful hands, large but manicured. His suit coat was open, so I could see how his perfectly fitted dress shirt hugged his muscles. He looked like he belonged on the cover of a magazine. I cannot remember the last time I scrutinized a man so thoroughly. Even though it was a bit unsettling being on a date at forty-five years old, there was a sense of confidence that I felt as an adult woman that I didn't have when I started dating Bryce. It was a strange, but exciting dichotomy of feelings racing through my head and my body.

It wasn't until I met Ian that I became cognizant of how I suppressed any sexual feelings in my body. I thought the sexual part of my being had passed away with my husband. I couldn't have been more mistaken. I had an ache between my legs that I thought had died a year ago. It was a relief to know that my body hadn't ceased to function. Unfortunately, this wasn't the appropriate time to be feeling turned on. I found myself squirming in my seat and squeezing my legs together to quell some of the tingling. He must have sensed that I was feeling a myriad of emotions, because he gave me the most devilish smile.

"A penny for your thoughts?" he said in a light and amusing tone. "OK, woman," I told myself, "This is it." Oh Christ, here it goes.

"I'm a little embarrassed by what I'm thinking," I said honestly.

"You should never feel anything but safe with me, Katharine. I will gladly admit that I'm smitten with you, and I would love to do all sorts of naughty things to you right now," he said with a smile so wide I swear his dimples winked at me. "I would like nothing more than to ravish every part of that delectable body of yours."

"So what's stopping you?" I asked him daringly. Holy cow, what was getting into me?

"My precious Katharine, the first time I make love to you will not be in a car, even if it is a limousine. I want to savor every part of you. It will happen slowly, and properly, in a very large bed. And I don't want to rush you into something you aren't ready for," he added compassionately.

"I think I'm becoming more ready by the minute," I said playfully. I finished off my glass of champagne and licked my lips seductively.

"Don't tempt me, counselor. We've only known each other a short time, and I'm having a very difficult time maintaining restraint as it is," he playfully scolded me.

I couldn't believe how much I liked it when he called me counselor. I thoroughly enjoyed the fact that he adopted a nickname for me so soon in our relationship. "I don't want to wait anymore. I want to be with you," I told him, as sincerely as I could. Holy crap, I couldn't believe how brazen I was being.

He leaned forward, took my hand, and kissed it gently. I felt shivers travel through my entire body. I lifted my hands and caressed his face. He had shaved, and his skin was very soft. I couldn't help but put my mouth on his cheek, then near his neck. I kept kissing him lightly. He let out a soft moan. I knew I was playing with fire, but I couldn't help it. I craved his touch, and I didn't want to wait. He grabbed the back of my head, careful not to mess up my hair, and pulled me into a deep, sensual kiss. I opened my mouth, and his tongue found mine. I loved the way he tasted. His teeth were smooth, and his breath was fresh. The champagne taste we shared made us taste like one. The ache between my legs was intensifying. We kissed for several minutes before he pulled back.

"I can't keep this up, Katharine. My attraction to you is becoming more obvious by the minute," he whispered in my ear. I glanced down at his lap. Oh God, his bulge was beautiful. I hadn't seen one of those in a very, very long time.

"I'm not sure I'll be able to keep a steady composure being next to you all night either," I shared. "I'm feeling very frustrated at the moment, and it's starting to feel almost painful. It has been quite a while, you know."

That was when he sat back and pulled my feet on his lap. He removed my shoes and started to rub my feet. I didn't have nylons on, so he was able to rub my skin. As he rubbed one foot, the other rested against his crotch, where I could feel him getting harder by the minute. It fueled my desire for him. I started to wiggle in my seat and squeeze my legs together even more tightly. I needed a way to release the frustration I was feeling.

"I think we both need to find some release before we go into the gala, or we'll never be able to function like respectable adults," he said.

"I'm feeling anything but respectable right now," I said in a low and breathy voice. His smile assured me that he wasn't feeling respectable either.

"I told you that the first time I make love to you will absolutely not be in a limo, but I think I can help us both out right now if you're game." I greedily nodded my consent, and he asked the driver to keep driving around until further notice. "I have a naughty idea that should make us both feel more comfortable. I'll show you mine if you show me yours."

"And how exactly shall we do that?"

He released my feet from his grasp, opened up his trousers, and pulled out his penis. It was big and hard and even more beautiful than I'd imagined. Holy crap, was this really happening? I took his cue and shimmied my dress up to my waist. Now, I felt embarrassed because I didn't have panties on, but it was too late to turn back now. I had never done anything like this before. It was so wanton. It made me pant with anticipation. Bryce and I had an amazing sex life, but we didn't do things like this. It was obvious that sex with Ian would be exciting and different. I felt like a giddy school girl in an adult body.

"No panties, counselor. How decadent of you," he said playfully.

"I didn't want to have panty lines, Mr. Jensen. It is always a point of contention for a woman. Nylons tend to be hot and always have the propensity to tear, and panty lines sully the look of a well-dressed woman. Thus, I made the conscientious decision to look as elegant as possible and leave the panties at home. On another note, I must say that you have quite an impressive member in your hands. I would love to get to know him better." Holy shit, where did that come from? I couldn't believe how bold I was being.

"All in good time, my lady. Right now, I'd like to see you touch yourself. I'll do the same. We need to release the tension so we can behave like proper adults at the gala. When the evening is over, if you are so inclined, I will let you do whatever you want with my member," he offered.

He started to pump his penis slowly and lovingly. It was killing me. I wanted to suck on it. I wanted to sit on it. I wanted him to slam it into me. But he was right; now wasn't the time for that. I started to rub my clit in circles. I felt like I was in some kind of porn movie. It was so incredibly naughty and so fucking hot. What the hell were we doing? We were two grown people who barely knew one another and we were simultaneously masturbating in the back of a limo! He continued to rub my feet with the hand that wasn't pumping his gorgeous body. I knew it wouldn't take me long to find my release. Obviously, he felt the same way.

"I'm ready when you are, counselor," he challenged.

I leaned my head back, closed my eyes, and came for the first time in months. When I started to recover, I stared as he came into the palm of his hand. When he started to relax, he pulled a handkerchief out of his breast pocket and wiped off his body. I realized at that moment that my body was also dripping wet. I looked down at my hand, and he knew exactly what I was thinking. He closed his pants quickly and came over to my side of the vehicle. He kissed me lightly behind my ear and on my neck and started wiping off my juices. He palmed my body with the cloth in his hand, massaging my clit in slow, loving circles. Oh my God, I couldn't believe how amazing that felt.

"One more time, counselor. You appear to have a lot of tension that you need to get a handle on."

He kept kissing my neck and ear as his touch became harder and more deliberate. My breath was ragged, and my heart was speeding up. He found my mouth and started to kiss me passionately. As I was getting closer, he put several fingers inside of me. That was all it took. I came long and hard. It was spectacular. He continued to kiss me until I came down from the incredible high. When I finally started to come down, he wiped the rest of my body off with his handkerchief so I would be more comfortable. It was a loving and considerate gesture. He helped me slide my dress back down over my hips. He rolled up the handkerchief and put it in a small trash receptacle. Our faces were inches apart. I gazed into his eyes and was blown away by everything I was feeling. I could feel his breath on my face. I should have been embarrassed by what had just transpired, but I wasn't. It felt so decadent; it felt so amazing. It was hard for me to find the right words to express what I was feeling.

"Thank you, Mr. Jensen. This was quite an impressive way to start our evening" was the best I could come up with.

"The pleasure was all mine, counselor."

16

The limousine ride was more thrilling than I could ever have expected. This woman was intoxicating. I knew I would never be able to get enough of her. It took us both a few minutes to compose ourselves. I slid back into my seat and advised my driver to take us to the gala. Katharine fixed her hair and put on more lipstick, I tucked my shirt in and fixed my bow tie, and we had another glass of champagne. Suddenly, Katharine started laughing.

"What's so funny?" I was curious to know what she was thinking.

"Oh gee, I don't know. How about the fact that two grown, respectable adults just simultaneously...well, you know? We both have pretty conservative careers, and what we just did was anything but conservative," she explained.

"Are you regretting what just happened?" I asked.

"Not at all. It's just funny that no matter how you portray yourself publically, you never know what happens behind closed doors."

"Well, I'm glad that you're comfortable with what transpired, because I found it quite exhilarating," I assured her.

"It was exciting. It was also naughty, and I think I've missed being naughty," she confessed to me with the most adorable smle on her face.

"It was a pleasure to bring some decadence into your life again. I hope there is a lot more where that came from."

After that exchange, we talked about nonsexual things, and our conversation was easy and unembarrassed. She was curious about my involvement in the gala.

"So what is your role in this event," she asked me.

"Once my mother was declared cancer-free, we established a non-profit organization called BIC or Believe in a Cure. We raise money for cancer victims and their families. It has been a huge success and the organization is growng every year. I don't have much of a hand's-on part of the operations anymore, but I always make sure that this event is a success. It is, by far, our largest fundraising event of the year," I said proudly.

"Well, I am honored to be a part of it," Katharine said sincerely.

At this point, a hint of our escapade was still lingering in the air, but we were adults. The sex (or nonsex) was hot as hell, but we both seemed very comfortable with how the situation played out. I felt a connection with Katharine that I hadn't thought I could feel with any woman.

When we walked into the entranceway of the theatre, my mom greeted us immediately.

"Who is this lovely lady, Ian?" she asked me pleasantly as I planted a quick kiss on her cheek, careful not to disrupt her makeup.

"Katharine Collins, this is my mother, Patricia Jensen. Mom, this is Katharine. Please be nice. We haven't been seeing each other very long, and I'm quite fond of her."

"Oh, I'm always nice, you silly boy. Katharine, you are a sight for sore eyes. Give me a little hug. I was afraid that horrid ex-wife had turned Ian against women forever. You are so lovely, my dear. What is it you do for a living?" she asked eagerly, obviously anxious for more information.

"I'm a partner at Stryder, Ross and Burton."

"A partner? That's impressive. I've worked with Doug Burton before. He's a top-notch attorney. Good for you, my dear. That's quite an accomplishment for such a young woman."

"I'm not as young as you think, but thank you, I appreciate the compliment. I love the firm, and I'm proud to be a part of it," Katharine said confidently.

"So where did you kids meet?" she continued. I could feel the whole twenty-question interrogation beginning. Besides, we were hardly kids.

"Mom, leave her alone already. We have the whole night for you to grill her. No more questions for now, please."

I was feeling a lot better now that the introduction was over with. It was obvious Katharine could hold her own in any situation, including in front of my mom. Thank God for that. My mother could be difficult and very protective. She knew I was a wealthy man, and she assumed every woman who showed interest in me was a gold digger like my ex-wife. For some reason, she was being unusually pleasant tonight. It unnerved me.

"Katharine, could you please excuse us for just a moment? I need to talk to Ian about a few boring details about tonight's gala."

"Of course not, Patricia. I'd actually like a moment to powder my nose."

Katharine gave me a little wink and was on her way. I imagined it wasn't her nose that needed to be "powdered." It was obvious that my mother was dying to say something to me, so I figured I would get her to spit it out as soon as Katharine was out of earshot.

"What's up, Mom?" I asked her.

"I'm so thrilled for you, Ian. Katharine is lovely. And she's an attorney? Oh my, that's wonderful. She must make a good living. She won't be after your money like that hussy you were married to."

"No, I'm confident she could care less about my money. Not only is she a successful attorney, she's also a widow. Her husband was a successful CPA in Manhattan who died last year of a massive heart attack. He was very young, and it was unexpected and extremely sudden. It has been a horrible year for her, and she is just starting to get out into the world again. She's really special, Mom. I like her a lot. Please be nice to her won't you? For me?" I begged her.

"I'll behave, darling. She seems lovely. I can feel the intensity between the two of you. It's exciting. And you are such a handsome couple. I'm rooting for you. It's about time you moved on from that money-hungry..."

"Mom, stop it. Here she comes," I pleaded with her.

The evening was a huge success. The food was excellent. The cash bar seemed to be thriving, which meant even more money would be raised for breast cancer. The band was energetic and quite talented. Katharine and I danced for a long time. Our bodies were in tune with each other, which made the night that much more enjoyable. We danced to every slow song, our bodies melting into each other with every beat. I couldn't help whispering naughty things in her ear and kissing her neck while we danced. Her body was very responsive, and I couldn't believe how much sexual tension we were both feeling. There was a silent auction toward the end of the evening that brought in a ton of money. All in all, the night was an incredible success. By the time we got back into the limo, it was well after midnight.

"Did you have a good time tonight?" I asked her.

"It was perfect. Thank you again for including me. I needed this more than I knew," she said reflectively.

"It was a wonderful evening for me as well. I can see you're exhausted, so I think I'll drop you off and let you get some sleep. Don't forget, I'm picking you up bright and early for the hike to Bear Mountain in the morning," I reminded her.

"Oh, I'd never forget. I hope the weather's nice. Some fresh air sounds wonderful." She stifled a yawn and I knew it was time to call it a night.

"Being with you is what sounds wonderful to me," I said to her honestly.

She didn't say anything; she didn't have to. She blushed and gave me the sweetest smile. There was definitely an intense sexual chemistry between us. But I wanted there to be so much more. Foreplay in the limo and dancing at the gala were both exhilarating, but I planned to be as patient as humanly possible with her. There didn't need to be any rush; I wanted this to be a long-lasting union.

We arrived at her place just before one in the morning. I could tell she was exhausted. Although I could have pulled an all-nighter with this exquisite beauty, I was respectful of her need to get some rest. I got out of the car and gave her a long, sensual kiss. She responded with such ardor that I could instantly feel my arousal. I knew that if I didn't walk away, I would have to walk her upstairs, and I was determined to behave. She needed some rest. Tomorrow was a new day.

"Goodnight, Katharine. Thank you for an incredible evening."

"Goodnight, Ian. Tonight was great. Thank you for including me."

17

Tonight was magical. We laughed and danced for hours, and I felt like I'd been reborn. Sadly, reincarnation was exhausting. I collapsed on my bed as soon as I was able to get my dress and shoes off. I didn't even bother to wash my makeup off; it could come off in the shower in the morning. I wanted to recap the evening in my mind, but I was too tired for that, too. So I sent a short text to Ian saying, "Thanks again—K" and fell into my deepest slumber in over a year.

I woke up bright and early to get ready for my day outdoors. Most people in New York walk everywhere since parking is so expensive and difficult to find. But walking in the city is just a means of getting from one place to another. You need to drive away from the city to enjoy the natural world. Fortunately, you never needed to drive far. New York state is very diverse, and there were a lot of wonderful places to go to get away from it all.

Ian was supposed to pick me up at nine, but I had already figured out that he liked to be early. And I was right. At 8:45 a.m., the intercom chirped. The doorman alerted me that Ian was downstairs waiting for me. I grabbed my backpack and hurried downstairs.

I had never seen Ian dressed casually. He looked heavenly in his Armani business suits. The tuxedo he'd worn last night had made him look even more divine. Today he was sporting a pair of jeans and a simple black T-shirt. This outfit was, by far, the sexiest to date. What was with this man? He was so beautiful. His jeans were worn, and his fitted black T-shirt accentuated his lean physique. I have always liked men dressed in black. How could a simple black T-shirt be such a turn on? He had black hiking boots on that made him look rugged. Holy crap, I was in trouble. This man was so hot. I really wanted to see him naked. Hiking could wait.

It was obvious that he'd just gotten out of the shower; his salt and pepper hair was messy and wet. Even that turned me on: I wished I could have been in the shower with him. I could have washed his hair. I could have washed other things...I needed to calm down. But if I could just grab his hair, stare into his eyes, and suck his face...This was not helping. I feel like my body has been invaded by a seventeen year old horny teenager.

"Good morning, counselor. What's going on in that beautiful head of yours?" he asked me mockingly as he walked towards me.

"I was thinking that it was nice to see you dressed casually," I said lightly. How did he know I was having perverse thoughts about him? He leaned into me and gave me a solid kiss on the lips. Holy crap, the kiss took my breath away.

"Is that all?" he asked seductively. Yep, I was busted. There was no way I was going to be able to conceal any of my emotions in front of this man.

"No, but it needs to be all, or we'll never make it out of the building," I admitted in defeat.

Ian laughed and kissed me again. He grabbed my bag and my hand, and we walked outside. His large hand held mine possessively. It felt incredible. I loved the strength and confidence he exuded. It made me safe and adored. He had a sports car waiting at the curb. It was not the vehicle I expected to drive us to the mountain. It was black, sleek, and very shiny.

"No driver today?" I asked him.

"No, I don't get many opportunities to drive my car, so I thought today would be a great day for it. I also wanted to be alone with you. This way we can talk about anything and not worry about being overheard."

"It's a beautiful car. It looks different from a normal corvette."

"It's a special edition; there weren't many made. I love how it handles. It has a big engine, which is useless in the city, so it's fun to drive out to the country with it. Are you ready?" he asked me.

"Sure am!"

The ride to Bear Mountain took a little over an hour. It was a clear, sunny day. It was still a little cool out, but it was supposed to warm up, and I knew the hiking would make me warm. We chatted comfortably. He was very proud of his daughters and told me more about their personalities and their lives. "Emily is more conservative than her younger sister. She has worked diligently in college to maintain a near perfect GPA so she can get into law school. She has been dating a fairly conservative young man for about a year now. His name is Martin. He seems like a nice enough fellow. They seem pretty serious, which makes me nervous. They're so young, you know?"

"You can't control when you fall in love Ian. Heck, I was only seventeen when I met Bryce. I always knew he was the one for me," I admitted honestly.

"Were you ever with anyone besides him?" he asked me. "Unless you'd prefer not to say. That's fine if you'd like to keep that information private. I don't mean to pry," he continued apologetically.

"No, it's a valid question. We both fooled around with other people our freshman year of college. I slept with a handful of guys. Every encounter was a disaster. I know Bryce slept with several girls. I think he may have fallen for one, but he would never talk about it. It was just a feeling I had at the time. In the end, we had a long-lasting, committed relationship. That was what was most important to me."

"You both were lucky for the time you had together," he remarked. He was very right about that. I know I was blessed, but that was not what I wanted to think about right now.

"Tell me more about Sara," I urged.

"She's a free spirit. She's a happy, vivacious young woman who doesn't have a clue what she wants out of life. For now, her main objective is to have fun. Honestly, as long as she maintains decent grades, I'm OK with that. I think you'll like her. She has a lot of spunk. I can't wait for you to meet both my girls. I have a feeling Emily will drill you with a million questions about your profession."

"Fine by me," I told him. "I wanted to be a lawyer for as long as I can remember. We will definitely have a lot to talk about. I look forward to meeting them both."

His enthusiasm for his children was endearing, and I responded by bragging about my son. He asked me several questions about Jackson. It was obvious that we were both interested in knowing more about each other's children. "Was it hard for Jackson to go away to college so shortly after his dad died?" he asked.

"Very. He didn't want to leave me, but I insisted. I didn't want my inability to cope with his father's passing to hold him back. His father and I were both so proud that he was accepted to Yale. I had to make him go. It helps that it isn't too far away. I wouldn't have been thrilled if he was off to California or Seattle. We talk on a regular basis, and he is enjoying his college experience. It was hard to see him leave, but I knew it was best for him."

"That was very noble of you, Katharine. It had to be very difficult for you to see him go. It shows how selfless you are and how much you love your son."

"Thank you Ian. I appreciate that."

I liked hearing about his daughters, and he seemed sincerely interested in knowing more about my son. Our kids were close in age, and I was glad for that. I think it would have been strange if he'd had small children; that would have changed the dynamics immensely. I'm sure I would have been willing to adapt to having younger children around, but I was relieved that I didn't have to. I hoped that someday our children could meet and possibly be friends.

We arrived at the mountain at 10:30 a.m. The sky was clear, and it had warmed up immensely. He parked his car in a parking lot next to a lodge, retrieved a backpack from the trunk, and we started to walk. I had never been to this area before, and I couldn't believe how breathtaking it was. We followed a trail for about an hour, and then Ian suggested we take a break at a picnic area that overlooked the river. He pulled out a bottle of white wine and poured two glasses.

"I thought we would celebrate," he said as he raised his glass to me.

"And what are we celebrating?" I asked.

"Two pimentos," he said with a huge grin.

I was so touched that he remembered the story I'd told him the first night we met; his toast brought tears to my eyes. It was obvious that he wasn't threatened by my husband's memory. It was such a loving thing to say.

"To two pimentos," I repeated, trying to maintain my composure. We clinked glasses, took a sip and sat back to enjoy the view.

After a few minutes, he reached into the backpack again. "I brought some snacks, too. I hope you like them." Ian unpacked Brie and crackers, grapes, and a selection of cured meats.

"Everything is perfect. Wine on top of a mountain with a handsome man is a lovely change of pace. It was thoughtful of you to bring a picnic. In the short time since we have met, I think I've already put a few of the pounds I lost back on, and it feels great."

"I'm so glad. I have more surprises, if you'll indulge me as the day progresses," he said.

"Really? It has been a long time since anyone surprised me with anything. I'm game for whatever you have in store for me," I told him.

"I'm so glad. I want you to feel safe, happy, and relaxed. Sound good?"

"Are you planning to spoil me, Mr. Jensen?"

"If you let me, counselor."

He leaned over and kissed me. I savored everything about this man. His strength. His smell. His taste. I was getting more smitten by the minute. When we finished the bottle of wine, we used the facilities and walked for another hour. We ended up at an inn located at the base of the mountain near where we had parked the car. I didn't realize there was a hotel here. It was such an awesome getaway for someone who lived in New York City. How had I never known about this place before? As we walked toward the front entrance of the inn, Ian took my hand.

"Ready for the next surprise?" he asked with the biggest grin.

"Bring it on," I told him.

He smiled. "Can you wait here while I grab our other bags from the car? I just want to make sure you have everything you need for afterward," he said mysteriously.

He was back by my side in less than five minutes. He must have sprinted to the car. He looked like a little kid as he approached me. His enthusiasm was infectious. We walked into the inn and toward what looked like an elegant spa. Ian told the receptionist that we had an appointment at two o'clock, and she directed us to a changing area.

"What are we having done?" I asked him. I really couldn't have cared less. I was just enjoying every minute of being with this man.

"A couples' massage. I thought it was about time you indulged in something nice. I'll meet you in the relaxation area once you've changed."

I locked my clothes in the locker and changed into a robe. I couldn't believe Ian had arranged all of this. It was so sweet and so thoughtful. No one had ever done something like this for me before. Whenever I'd thought about getting a massage or facial, Bryce would tell me to schedule something. This was such an unexpected surprise. I could totally get used to all of this attention.

We met in the common waiting area and sat next to each other on a couple's couch. It was obviously a meditative kind of room, where one was expected to be quiet. Fortunately, we were alone in the room. He held my hand. His touch made me feel giddy. There was soft music in the background and a fire in the corner of the room. We each had a glass of water with a slice of cucumber in it. "Have you been to the spa before?" I asked him quietly. "No," he said. "I tried to get Monica to come here once, but she said she hated the outdoors. I told her about the spa, and she insisted we go to one of the swanky ones in the city. It wasn't worth fighting over." It made me so sad that his marriage was so unhappy. "What a shame," I told him. "So, have you stayed at the lodge before?" I wanted to know. "Yes. Once. I had a business conference here years ago. That was how I discovered the place. I've brought the girls here before to hike, but we've never spent the night. We have eaten in the restaurant, and the food is excellent," he told me. I wanted to get closer to him, so I rested my head on his shoulder and he put his arm around me. Neither of us spoke again as we gazed at the fire. It felt good to relax. It had been such a long time.

After ten minutes, a woman in a black uniform walked into the waiting area and escorted us into a room where we were left alone to undress and get on our respective massage tables. We had never seen each other naked before, and I felt shy. My body didn't look the same as it did when I was younger. Even though I was thin, I didn't feel fit anymore. I was lucky that I didn't have stretch marks from being pregnant, but I still felt less confident about my body. Moreover, no man had seen me naked aside from my husband since I was eighteen years old. It was no wonder I was feeling ill at ease. It was obvious that I was hesitant about disrobing in front of him. I stood there, unsure of which direction to face. I just looked at Ian, waiting for some kind of cue. Sensing my hesitation, Ian walked over to me. He cupped his hands on my face and gave me the most loving kiss.

"Don't be embarrassed, Katharine. After the limo, this should be easy."

He made a valid point. I leaned back from his kiss and removed my robe. He did the same. We just stared at each other. The last thing I wanted was a massage. I wanted this man. It was obvious by the change in his body how much he wanted me, too. His reaction to seeing me naked made me feel more confident.

"We better lie down before we get in trouble," he suggested with a naughty laugh. I started to laugh with him and scooted onto the table as quickly as possible. I didn't want either one of us to be embarrassed when the massage therapists entered the room.

The massages were excellent; I felt incredibly relaxed. When they ended, we got up and put our robes back on. Ian walked over to me and enveloped me in his arms. It was such a strong and loving hug. He didn't try to kiss me. He played with my hair with one hand and held my body with his other. I just held my arms around his back, enjoying the feel of his strong, warm body. I closed my eyes tightly so I could enjoy every sensation I was feeling.

"Thank you so much for this, Ian." I opened my eyes, leaned back, and looked into his.

"You're most welcome. I don't want to pressure you into anything, but I have another surprise. If you aren't ready for it, just say the word—I have a backup plan. Either way, I just want to be with you."

"So what's the next surprise?" I asked him excitedly.

"I've reserved a room here. We can go upstairs and relax before dinner. If that makes you uncomfortable, we can always go to dinner now and head back to the city tonight."

I took his hand in mine and said, "Lead the way upstairs, Mr. Jensen." And that is exactly what he did.

Still in our robes, we grabbed our clothes from our respective lockers and handed them to a porter, who showed us the way to our room. We went upstairs to a beautiful suite with a spectacular view. There was Prosecco on ice and a tray of snacks on a dining table. Ian poured us both a glass, and we sat on the veranda snacking and chatting. It was unbelievable how comfortable I was with this man—I had known him less than a week. "Did you and your husband go on many romantic getaways," he asked me. "Not locally," I told him. "We enjoyed traveling to Europe on vacations. Even when Jackson was born, we traveled to Europe. What about you and Monica?" He sat quiet for a moment and had a forlorn look on his face. "We went on a few trips when we were first married, like Vegas and Napa Valley. I thought we were happy and in love, but it didn't last long. Once she had Emily, everything changed. She was miserable. Looking back on it, I guess it was postpartum. Then she got pregnant with Sara and nothing was ever the same again. She complained all of the time about being sick or fat. It was like she was making a huge sacrifice having children. I heard rumors about women loving the process of being pregnant and being thrilled about nursing the baby. That is not how it was in our house. She complained incessantly throughout the entire pregnancy. Hell, she never considered nursing either of the girls. She didn't want the shape of her breasts to change. I don't know why it mattered. She got her boobs done anyways after Sara was born anyways. I never realized how selfish she was until after we divorced. I'm sorry about how everything turned out, but I am beyond grateful for my girls."

I liked the fact that he felt comfortable enough opening up to me about his relationship with his ex-wife. It showed more of his character, which made me feel even closer to him. We were older. We both had life experiences that shaped who we were and what we wanted out of life. And we both had a past. It was important we could be honest with one another about our previous relationships. So far, he had been extremely forthcoming. And so had I.

It felt very intimate, sitting on the veranda with our luxurious robes on, but I wasn't nervous or uncomfortable at all. If anything, I was excited about our evening. I loved the fact that Ian had planned the day so thoroughly. He was a very thoughtful man, which I found very endearing. It was pretty obvious where this adventure was leading, and I couldn't wait to enjoy every minute of it.

18

I felt like a child on Christmas morning. I had planned the week-end down to the smallest detail, but I didn't know if she would think it was too soon to spend the night together. I did have a back-up plan in case she wasn't ready yet. It made me so happy that she was enjoying herself. There was no reason this fascinating woman should have to live another day in such a solitary existence. I was overjoyed that she was willing to continue with the plans that I had made. I forgot how rewarding it was to spoil a woman. I always enjoyed organizing surprises for people I cared about, but I hadn't been able to do it for a romantic interest in nearly twenty years.

After we sat on the veranda for a while, I asked her if she was interested in taking a bath with me. There was an oversized Jacuzzi tub in the room, and I had made sure there were lavender bath salts for the tub and candles I could light to enhance the ambiance. She said she would love to take a bath. I was thrilled at how easygoing and receptive she was. She disappeared into the bathroom, and I lit the candles. I also refilled our champagne glasses and set them next to the tub as I started to fill it. I added the salts, and the scent immediately filled the air. I slipped into the tub before she emerged from the bathroom, so there would be no awkwardness.

She smiled when she saw me in the tub and dropped her robe to the floor so I could look at her.

"No other man has seen me naked in almost thirty years," she said quietly.

"I'm honored to be the one to be looking at you now. You're a very beautiful woman, Katharine."

She climbed into the tub opposite me and leaned back to rest her head against the headrest. I handed her the glass of Prosecco and turned the jets on. We sat in silence for a few minutes with our legs entwined. I rubbed her foot with my free hand. Being in the tub together naked was even more erotic than I'd imagined.

I needed to touch her, so I leaned forward to caress her face. She had put her hair in a ponytail, which made her look young and carefree. There was a stray hair hanging over her cheek, so I pushed it behind her ear and proceeded to rub the front of her shoulders. She tilted her head back and moaned. I knew that she missed being touched, and I needed to be the one who touched her. It felt so good to be the one to give her what she needed. The more I rubbed the sides of her neck and shoulders, the more she relaxed.

"That feels amazing, Ian. Thank you for arranging all of this. I could get used to being spoiled."

"It has been my pleasure. You know, I haven't been able to spoil a woman in many years. I was worried that I had forgotten how to do it. It was a lot of fun planning this weekend. Believe it or not, it pleases me as much as it is pleasing you."

"I find that hard to believe, but I'll take your word for it. You've done more for me in less than a week than all of my therapy sessions this year did. Saying thank you just doesn't seem like enough," she said reflectively.

"Your happiness is payment enough, Katharine. I want to savor every moment we have together."

She opened her eyes and stared into mine. I felt such a longing for this woman. She grabbed my face and pulled me closer to her. She found my mouth. Her kisses started out slowly but quickly became intense.

She began to bite my tongue and my lips, and I could feel my body getting even more aroused. I kissed her back with the same amount of passion. We began to grope one another. Her body was so soft and sexy. Her hands were all over me, like she was memorizing my body. As our breathing became rapid and our kisses became more ardent, I sat back and pulled her on top of my lap.

My midsection rested against her core. I continued to kiss her and fondle her scrumptious breasts. She ran her hands through my hair and continued to kiss me passionately. When she noticed how hard I was beneath her. she started moving her body back and forth over mine. I held onto her hips while she began her dance. It felt so good—I wanted so much more. We kissed and stroked and said naughty things to one another. And we laughed. It felt so good to laugh with her. Katharine was flushed, and her nipples were as hard as rocks. I was telling her how much I wanted to bury my body deep inside of her when she let out a stifled moan; I watched her face change as her orgasm consumed her. The look on her face, and the friction of our bodies rubbing together, was all it took for me to join her.

I couldn't believe we'd both had an orgasm just by rubbing against one another. I felt like a teenager having a heavy make-out session. I had forgotten how much fun it was to make-out with a girl. It was so erotic. When our breathing became more normal and our heartbeats slowed down, I asked Katharine if she was ready for a nap. She nodded, smiled at me, and gave me a long, sensual kiss. We stood in the tub. I wrapped a towel around her, picked her up, and carried her to the bed.

I dried myself off and climbed in next to her. She laid on her side, so I spooned her. She grabbed my hand and kissed it. I felt elated by our connection, but I also felt exhausted by the enormity of what was happening between us. I pulled the covers completely over our bodies and began to lovingly stroke her hair. Before I knew it, we were both sound asleep.

19

I woke up confused, not sure where I was. I looked up and saw that the clock said six. I took note of my surroundings and realized that Ian's hand was on my stomach and one of his legs was draped over mine. His other hand was tangled in my hair. I could tell he was still asleep, but I felt compelled to look at him.

I slowly adjusted my position in bed so I was face-to-face with him. It was fascinating to watch him sleep. It turned me on to see him looking so peaceful. OK, everything about this man turned me on. I touched his chest with my hand. His body was so hard, but the curls of his chest hair were so incredibly soft. I started caressing his chest, and he opened his eyes.

"Hey there, counselor, having a good time?" he teased me.

"I am. You have a beautiful chest. I was just admiring it."

"You also have a beautiful chest that I would like to take a minute to admire."

He reached down and started caressing my breasts. I moaned with pleasure. He lowered his mouth to my body and started sucking on my nipples. I was so turned on. I'd had three orgasms since I met this man, and none of them had been through penetration. I was pretty sure that if he kept sucking my breasts like this, I was ready to combust yet again. I felt excited, and a little bit nervous. It had been so long since I was with another man besides my husband, but for some reason, this felt right.

"Stop thinking, Katharine, and enjoy what I'm giving you," he said seductively. How did he know I was analyzing our foreplay?

His voice and his mouth were all it took to send me over the edge. Between the way he devoured my breasts, the positioning of our intertwined legs, and the friction of our midsections rubbing against one another, I was able to climax with ease. It was incredible—number four, just like that. Since when had I started counting orgasms? Probably since I hadn't had that many in over a year. I was feeling guilty about coming by myself when I felt something hot and wet against my leg. He had come with me.

I started to laugh. "Is something funny?" he asked me with a wicked smile on his face.

"I feel like a horny teenager," I told him, still laughing.

"So do I. It's been way too long since I felt like this, " he said to me with the most beautiful grin on his face.

"Who would have thought making out could be so much fun? Still, I really want you inside me," I confessed.

"I've enjoyed playing with you, too, Ms. Collins. But our playtime will have to wait until later, because we have a dinner reservation in twenty minutes. You need to keep your strength up so you can handle what I have in store for you later."

"Is that a promise, Mr. Jensen?"

"It sure is, so let's get this food thing over with so we can get back to bed."

"OK. I'm actually very hungry, so let's motivate."

We got up and got dressed; I was glad I had brought an outfit that would be appropriate for dinner. He put some music on and we got ready in a comfortable silence. A lot had happened in the past week, and it seemed like we were both lost in our own heads. There was nothing awkward about it, though. It felt like I had known him for a lot longer than five days.

Dinner was delicious. We had no problem finding things to talk about. Anyone listening to our conversation would have thought we'd been friends for years. At one point, we started talking about our in-laws. "Bryce's parents are having the most difficult time dealing with his dealth. I call them every week. So does Jackson. We see them every couple of months, but it is so difficult being with them. They have aged so much in the past year," I told him. "Like you had?" he reminded me. "Yes, like I had. Until I met you." I responded nostalgically. "Have you kept in touch with Monica's parents?" I wondered. "Not really. They talk to the girls once in awhile. I know they aren't mad at me, but it is still awkward. Honestly, I think they are embarrassed. Their daughter had a loving husband, two great daughters and anything she could want, and then she threw it all away for a guy at the gym." I shook my head in disgust. "She's an idiot," was all I could say.

We also talked about our own parents. He told me how difficult his mother's cancer was on the entire family. His father took it especially hard. He said that his dad was really scared his wife was going to die. He stayed by her side through the surgery and every treatment she had. It sounded like his parents had a great relationship. Ian told me that it was such a relief when they were told she was in remission.

I told him how sad my folks were when Bryce died. They loved him like a son. But after a few months passed, they were more worried about me. They called me constantly, but I wouldn't answer their calls most of the time. It was hard to talk to them without crying. I would send messages that said I was swamped with work and didn't have the time to talk. Of course, that was a lie. I just didn't have the strength to pretend I was doing well. I didn't do a very good job hiding my despair. They were extremely concerned with how poorly how I was handling his death. In retrospect, they had a definite reason to be concerned.

As the dinner progressed, I found myself falling into a natural rhythm with this man. It was getting easier to leave the memory of Bryce in another part of my brain. I was fascinated with Ian and wanted to get to know him better. I cannot believe how self-absorbed I had been over the past year. This was so refreshing, focusing on someone else for once. Several times during dinner, he reached for my hand. I could feel a spark every time he did. The connection between us was very intense, and I felt like a starving woman who couldn't get enough food. His touch felt like the only thing that could satiate me.

After we finished dinner, Ian suggested we go for a walk. It was a beautiful evening. There was a nearly full moon and a sky full of stars. We walked along a path next to the river, holding hands. I felt safe and comfortable with this man. About twenty minutes into the walk, we sat down on a large, canvas swing that was big enough for two people. He put his arm around me, and we cuddled. I loved the feel of his muscles and couldn't help but run my hand over his chest. When I touched his nipples through his shirt, I felt them get hard. That stirred something wonderful between my legs. As I nestled my head in the crook of his shoulder, I looked down and could see him getting harder. I could sense he was waiting for me to make the move. He said several times that he didn't want to rush me.

"Can we go back to the room? I asked him pleadingly.

"Are you sure you're ready for this?" he asked.

"I don't think I've ever been more sure of anything in my life."

20

I was waiting for Katharine to make the first move. Even though we'd had a few erotic make out sessions, making love was different. I needed her to be completely ready for it. I couldn't risk her feeling pressured by me or regretting her decision. I knew what I wanted: I wanted to make love to her for hours. But I also knew I wanted more than a one-night stand. I could see myself with her for a long time, and I wasn't about to mess it up.

We walked back to the room holding hands. I loved the way her small hand fit in mine. I couldn't wait for her hands to be all over my body. There was a bottle of Courvoisier waiting for us; it was one of my favorite after-dinner drinks, but I didn't know if she liked it or not. I pointed to it to see if she was interested and she smiled. I poured two snifters and handed one to her.

"To a magical night with a beautiful woman," I toasted her.

"I'll toast to that," she said with a large grin.

We sat on the veranda for a short while, admiring the view and chatting. She told me how she'd never thought she would be with a man again. That made me sad. She was only in her forties. "We were together for almost thirty years, Ian. And it was a great marriage. How could I ever expect to find that kind of love again?" she asked me rhetorically. I had to believe in second chances, so that is what I told her. "I don't think you can put a limit to how much love is in your heart. Whether you have one child or ten, you'd still love them all, right? I think you just need to open up your heart and give love a chance. Do you think you'll be able to do that Katharine?" I asked her, anxious for the answer I was hoping to hear. "I think I already have," she said.

It must have been terrible for her to think she would be alone for the rest of her life. She admitted that her relationship with her husband had been so wonderful that she didn't think she could ever find that kind of connection with another person again. I teased her about the pressure that put on me, and she apologized profusely. That made me laugh. "For an attorney who loves to argue and debate, you are quite easy to tease. And I love to see you blush. It's very endearing," I told her. I assured her that a relationship with me would be different, but it could also be wonderful. I'd never want her to forget what she'd had with her husband. If he hadn't died, they would still be together. But he had, and for some reason, fate had brought us together. I didn't believe that people were meant to be alone—if you opened your heart, you never knew what you might find. I had always hoped I would fall in love again, even if I didn't think it would ever happen. I admired that level of commitment that she had with him. Hell, I wish my wife had honored our vows and stayed committed to me. Sadly, I couldn't control her actions and our divorce was inevitable. It was a pretty serious conversation, but it felt comfortable to talk about this kind of stuff with her.

I admitted to her that I'd felt pretty stymied in the relationship department after my wife had cheated on me. Her infidelity had hurt me in more ways than I could even describe. I had believed in the vows we took, and her betrayal felt like a knife tearing me apart—not only in my heart, but in my soul as well. She had destroyed our family and my faith in the sanctity of marriage. I told Katharine about the few short-term flings I'd had over the past few years. They had been purely physical, because I was too afraid to open myself up again and get hurt. "It's incredible how my body would feel an intense need for sex, and then it would be unfulfilling because there was no emotion included. I found myself spending more time at the gym to quell my primal needs. The past few years have been really difficult. Monica really did a number on me. I was skeptical about feeling safe enough to try again," I admitted to her. I really was paranoid about opening up my heart to the possibility of love again. Until now. Katharine made me feel safe. I'd thought it would be hard to expose how vulnerable I felt, but I could tell that Katharine understood and felt compassion for me. It was very comforting. "I'm not going to lie," I had to put all my cards on the table, "I never thought I'd fall for someone as hard as I am falling for you. It's exciting. and it's terrifying. I feel like I am in the most wonderful dream that I hope I never wake up from." A tear escaped from her eye when I shared my pain and admitted my intense attraction to her. I wiped the tear away and thanked her for listening.

She didn't say anything. She stood up, took my hand, and walked me into the bedroom. We started to undress each other slowly, taking in every inch of each other's bodies. Her body was breathtaking. I couldn't tell that she had ever had a baby. She was firm in all the right places and soft where a woman should be soft. My hands roamed everywhere, from her neck to her shoulders, and all the way down. I kissed her lightly, but she wanted more. She raised herself on her toes, grabbed the back of my head, and pulled me in closer to her. Our kissing intensified, and our hands wandered. Suddenly, she leaned back and laughed.

"I'm too short to do this standing. Could we please lie down?"

She didn't need to ask me twice. I scooped her up and gently put her down on the bed. My arousal was obvious, but I wanted to savor every minute with her. I laid next to her with only one leg over hers so I could admire her body. I kissed her mouth ardently; I loved the taste of her. I couldn't help myself, though—I needed to explore. I kissed her neck and sucked on her ear, and she let out a moan that fueled my desire for her. I moved down and found her breasts. They were exquisite. As I feasted on them, her nipples became hard, and her hips wiggled against me, looking for more friction. The more I sucked on her nipples, the more sounds escaped from her lips. I continued loving her breasts with my mouth and one of my hands, while the other hand traveled down to feel between her legs. She was soaking wet. I needed to know what she tasted like.

I nestled myself comfortably between her legs. Her scent was intoxicating. She had a small patch of hair in the front, but she had gotten rid of all the hair on her lips. I couldn't believe how much I enjoyed her scent and her taste. She played with my hair as I feasted on her body. I could feel her lips swelling under my tongue as I kissed and licked every part of her. I couldn't seem to get enough, and it was obvious that she loved it, too. She begged me to apply more pressure. Before I knew it, she was screaming my name and exploding in my mouth.

21

"That felt so good, Ian. Thank you so much!" I gasped.

"You are very welcome. Believe me, the pleasure was all mine. Hopefully that will be the first of many," he said smugly.

"God, I hope so!"

He chuckled and started making his way up my body, kissing and touching me everywhere. When he finally made it to my neck, I begged him to put himself inside me. He slid off of me for a quick second and put a pillow under my hips. I preferred to have my hips elevated, and he somehow seemed to know that's how I would like it. It made the angle that much better. I already felt appreciation for his oral skills. Now I had a very strong feeling he was going to impress me this way as well.

He entered me slowly, but at this point, I needed him to be rough, not gentle. It had been such a long time, and this man had my juices flowing in more ways than one. I begged him to give me all that he had. When he did, I was startled. He was bigger and thicker than Bryce had been. It didn't hurt; it just surprised me at first. Sensing my hesitation, he asked if he was hurting me. I assured him that the only thing that would hurt me was if he stopped. He started moving again, and I couldn't believe how much I missed the sensation of having a man inside of me again. We found the most perfect rhythm. He had one hand behind my neck and the other one on my breast. I had both of my hands digging into his ass and pushing him harder toward me. I missed this feeling. It was heaven. As his breathing became more labored, he started whispering in my ear. He urged me to swallow every ounce of his body with mine. I loved how his voice changed and got even deeper as he kept saying erotic things to me. I couldn't last another minute. I yelled for him to join me; that is exacty what he did. They say it's unusual for a couple to climax at the same time during penetration, but our timing was impeccable, which made it all the more intense.

Our breathing started to slow, and Ian found my mouth once again. He kissed me lovingly. He made me feel adored. It was wonderful. My body felt satiated in a way that I'd needed more than I even knew. I ran my fingers through his hair and forced him to look at me.

"That was incredible, Ian. I feel so grateful for you right now," I told him sincerely.

"I feel the same way, Katharine. I had pretty much given up on this happening to me. I'm so glad I was wrong. You are such a gift."

He rolled over on his back and pulled me close to him. My head rested on his chest, and I could hear his heart beat. We were both tired and content. Before I could think about anything else, I was sound asleep.

22

Making love to Katharine was better than I could ever have imagined. Her body was beautiful, and I loved how she responded to me. I have never felt such a connection with a woman before, not even my wife. I felt so blessed to have met her.

When she cuddled up next to me, I couldn't help touching her. I rubbed her back and her head. Before I knew it, she was sound asleep. I watched her for a while. She looked like an angel sleeping beside me. It didn't take long for me to join her in a happy slumber.

I was dreaming about Katharine sucking on me, a beautiful dream that I didn't want to end. Except it wasn't a dream. I woke up to her taking every inch of me into her mouth. No woman had ever been able to take it all in before, and it was a magnificent feeling. When I opened my eyes, she was looking at me with a grin.

"Enjoying yourself, Katharine?" I asked her.

"Sure am," she sputtered, resuming her task.

She sucked every part of me while her hands worked their magic. She licked me gently and sucked me hard. There was nothing predictable about what she was doing; she kept me guessing. That made all of the sensations that much more intense. I knew I wouldn't last long, and I told her so. She just smiled and kept sucking. Before long, I exploded in her mouth. She lapped up every drop. Our adventure just kept getting better.

When my spasms had stopped, she crawled up my body and lay on top of me, whispering all sorts of pleasantries in my ears. I relished every sensation I was experiencing. I rubbed my hands up and down her body. We began making out like horny teenagers again, and I loved how passionate she was. It didn't take long for me to get aroused again, and before I knew what was happening, Katharine was straddling my legs and sitting on top of me. Her tight body felt amazing as it engulfed every ounce of me. She wanted control, and I had no desire to argue with her. She set the pace, which started out slowly and increased as our arousal did. I held her hips and helped her ride me. As she was getting close, she laid her chest on mine and kissed me hungrily. "Join me," she invited, and that was all it took. Once again, we climaxed in unison. It was magical.

"I could get used to waking up next to you every morning," I told her when I could finally catch my breath.

"I think that would please me greatly, Mr. Jensen," she said.

"First, though, can we order some breakfast? I'm famished."

23

I don't even know how long I layed there staring at him when I woke up. He was one of the best-looking men I had ever seen. His body couldn't have been more perfect, either. But it was all of the other things that really attracted me to him. I loved how he'd arranged the weekend with such detail, and also how he'd allowed me to decide whether or not we stayed the night. He was so thoughtful and caring. I found his thoughtfulness even hotter than his perfectly chiseled physique. I loved how bright he was, and how we never lacked for something to talk about. I couldn't believe he'd come into my life. Part of me was still waiting to wake up from this beautiful dream.

My intellectual adoration only lasted for so long before my body was craving him even more. I loved waking him up like I did, and it was obvious that he enjoyed it as well. I was surprised that I didn't feel more inhibited with him, but I didn't. He made me feel comfortable and beautiful. I prayed he was really as wonderful as he seemed, because I was falling fast and hard.

We had omelets, fresh fruit, and coffee for breakfast. We talked about how passionate our lovemaking had been, and I was so happy that he felt the connection as strongly as I did. We agreed that we needed to spend a lot more time in bed. I had never talked to a man so openly about sex.

It felt naughty. It also felt liberating. Sex was so much fun with him. I'd forgotten how much I missed it.

He told me we had the option to hike, swim, or fish today. I wasn't interested in any of the above and asked him how long we had the room for. He laughed and told me he had already asked for a late checkout, just in case. We had the room until four in the afternoon; it was only ten in the morning now. I was excited to have six more hours alone with this remarkable man.

Once the decision was made, he picked me up and carried me back to bed. I loved the way he kept picking me up. It made me giggle every time. We tried a different position with every round. His physical strength turned out to be a lot of fun in bed too. There are definitely advantages to having sex with a physically fit man. He also had incredible stamina. That must have been another benefit of his excellent physical fitness, which I thoroughly enjoyed and took total advantage of. I knew I needed to start working out again so I could keep up with him.

Before we knew it, it was closing in on four o'clock. I didn't want this day to end. He had turned a simple hike into a magnificent weekend. I felt relaxed and happy; Ian was rocking my world, and I was enjoying every minute of it. There was a part of me that couldn't believe everything that was happening. The attorney side of my brain was always skeptical, however.

"You seem to be too good to be real. Fess up Jensen, are you a serial killer, child molestor or what?" I asked him jokingly.

"You want the truth counselor? I am a grown man who resigned myself to spending the rest of my life as a single man. Then one day, I saw a woman sitting alone at a bar crying. A little voice urged me to talk to her. Thank God I listened to that voice. Less than one week later, my world has turned upside-down, and I have found myself completely and utterly smitten with this beautiful vixen who has entered my life. I abhor violence and I could never hurt a child, so you are safe. The only thing you should be frightened of is the depth of my feelings for you."

"Wow, I didn't expect that. Your soliloquy seems very genuine, and I am flattered by your compliments." I paused for a minute to digest everything he had said before I continued. "No, your feelings don't frighten me Ian; they excite me. I am extremely grateful that you approached me the other evening. I also felt a little voice urging me to accept your invitation to dinner. I don't know if it was divine intervention, or simply a coincidence, but I am pleased it happened. I haven't felt sunshine in over a year. You brought that bright, warm light back into my life. I feel like Prince Charming finally found me."

Our drive back to the city was fairly quiet; we were both worn out from our crazy day in bed. He held my hand the whole way, except when he was forced to change gears. When he let go of me, I put my hand on his thigh. I couldn't stop myself from touching him.

As he pulled up in front of my apartment, I felt a little sad. I didn't want to come down from my euphoria. Even though it hadn't even been a week, the thought of spending the night without him seemed so lonely. I wanted to ask him to stay, but I didn't want to seem needy. He must have been feeling the same way, because he asked me if I wanted to order some takeout before we called it a night. His suggestion made me giddy. We gave the car keys to the doorman and went up to my place. I asked what his preferences for takeout were, and he told me to surprise him. I ordered from my favorite Thai place. They said it would take an hour.

Since we had time to kill, I opened up a bottle of wine and handed him a glass. My cat was thrilled that I was home, so I fed her and gave her some love. I escorted Ian into my living room and lit a fire. We chatted about the weekend and more about our kids. His older daughter was graduating from American University in Washington in May; she planned to go to law school in the fall. His other daughter was a sophomore at Fordham University here in New York; she wasn't sure what she wanted to do yet. She was good in math and sciences, he said, so she was thinking about going into medicine. I was impressed that his girls were bright. It shouldn't have surprised me, since I'd discovered that Ian was a financial genius. Investments and stocks were a fun game that he played, and he played them well. He owned stock in dozens of thriving companies. I was so impressed with his financial savvy. He admitted that he felt like a big kid playing monopoly. He said he was lucky, but it was obvious that there was more than luck involved.

I told him how Jack had followed in our footsteps and was going to Yale. He had decided to study business, but he wasn't really sure what he wanted to do. He wasn't interested in law or accounting like his parents. He wasn't very good in the sciences, so medicine was out, too. He had always been drawn to marketing campaigns and clever advertising, so he was hoping to get an internship over the summer with some kind of advertising firm.

It shouldn't have surprised me when Ian told me he was part owner of a thriving advertising firm that had been established about five years ago. He said he knew for a fact that they hired interns to do a lot of the grunt work during the summers, since that was their busiest season. He offered to help Jack secure an internship with the company if he was interested. I couldn't thank him enough. I told him I'd call Jack and see what he thought, but I knew exactly what he would think: he would freak out.

Then it occurred to me that I could offer the same for his daughter Emily. She had already been accepted into law school, and she wanted to work in a law office over the summer. I didn't think it was a good idea for her to work with me, but there were hundreds of other attorneys wanting interns. I shared my thoughts with Ian, and he was as pleased as I had been by his offer to help my son.

The Thai food came, and we ate on the floor in front of the fire. Fortunately, he liked spicy food—the owner of the restaurant knew I liked my food hot. Ian seemed to enjoy the food as much as I did. When we finished eating, it was obvious that we were both tired. He put his arm around me, and we leaned back against the couch. I put my head on his shoulder. It felt so good to have him here.

"I don't want you to go home tonight," I said wearily.

"I don't either."

"Please don't go. I have to be at work by eight tomorrow morning, but I'd love for you to stay."

"I have to be at work just as early. If I leave at seven, I can run back to my place, put a suit on, and be ready to conquer the world in time for my morning meeting."

"How about a shower before bed?" I suggested.

"Lead the way, counselor."

24

We didn't get much sleep, but I couldn't have cared less. We made love in the shower, and then in the bed. I woke up around three in the morning to her hand wrapped tightly around me, which led to another round. When my alarm went off at six, she wasn't in the bed. I walked into the kitchen to find her pouring us coffee and singing to Anita Baker. Katharine had a beautiful voice, and she looked so happy.

I came from behind her and hugged her tightly. She had an over-sized Yale T-shirt on, and nothing else. I couldn't help groping her; she looked so fucking sexy in her T-shirt. She swung around, put her arms around my neck, and started kissing me. I lifted her up and set her on the counter. She wrapped her legs around my waist. It didn't take long for my body to respond to her. She used her toes to wiggle my boxers down. It had only been a few hours since we'd made love, but we were both ready to go at it again. Once she freed me from my boxers, she grabbed the part of my body she was interested in, and positioned it right where she wanted it. I needed to see her naked, so I pulled off her shirt in one quick swoop and started to suck on her gorgeous tits. She leaned her head back against the cupboard and pulled my hair. I loved it when she did this—it felt so raw and sexy. She met my frenzied speed, thrusting her hips in sync with mine. It didn't take either of us very long to reach our climax. It was so hot, having sex with her on her kitchen counter. A guy could really get used to this.

I pulled out of her and grabbed the kitchen towel to wipe us off. I didn't want our juices running all over the kitchen floor. After I finished drying her, she kissed me on the lips and offered me coffee. We took our coffee into the bedroom, and I sat on her bathroom counter while she started putting on makeup and doing her hair. Hanging out with her while she did her morning routine seemed very natural, like we had been doing it for years.

I hated the thought of leaving her, so I invited her to dinner. She said she had to work late, but she would be ready around eight. I offered to pick her up at work, and she agreed. I saw that it was almost seven and knew I had to get going. I called down for the doorman to retrieve my car, got dressed, and hugged her for the longest time. We thanked each other for the weekend, and I forced myself to leave.

I called my daughter Emily when I knew she wasn't in class and told her about Katharine's offer of an internship at Stryder the following summer. She was elated. Then she started with a barrage of questions about Katharine. I told her that the relationship was very new, but that I was crazy about her. Holy crap, I'd just admitted that to my daughter. I told Emily that we'd gone to Bear Mountain; the girls loved hiking there. She asked me if we'd spent the night at the inn, and I had to be honest with her. It was a pact we'd made after their mother had lied to all of us for so many years. Emily seemed genuinely pleased and said she couldn't wait to meet the new lady in my life. I liked the thought of introducing Katharine to my girls.

I couldn't wait for dinner, so I arrived at her firm around seven-thirty and took the elevator to her floor. There was a receptionist sitting at the desk at the entrance to her office. I introduced myself as Ian Jensen and told her I had a dinner engagement with Mrs. Collins. The girl gave me the biggest smile and introduced herself to me. Her name was Suzie. She shook my hand and told me it was a pleasure to meet me. Then she thanked me for putting a smile back on her boss's face. Well, I guess I wasn't a secret. That pleased me immensely—her acknowledgment made me blush, and I didn't know I was capable of blushing at my age. I told her that it was my pleasure: her boss had a beautiful smile, and she deserved to smile more often. She picked up her phone to alert Katharine of my early arrival, and the door of her office opened immediately. She was, by far, the sexiest attorney I had ever seen. She had a fitted navy pinstripe skirt with a matching blazer, a white blouse that accentuated her breasts, and high heels that made her legs that much sexier. Her hair was up in a twist, and she had a pair of glasses on. I was blown away all over again. How could anyone look that hot in fucking pinstripes? She walked toward me and gave me a kiss. I was glad she approached me, because I was frozen to my spot. She told the receptionist to go home, took my hand, and led me into her office. She closed the door quietly behind us. I couldn't help myself: I pushed her up against the door and started kissing her passionately. When she could finally get some air, she teased me about being happy to see her. I told her how hot she looked and how badly I wanted to throw her on her desk and fuck her senseless. Although she agreed that sex on the desk was an excellent idea, she told me that the cleaning crew came into the office every evening around eight to vacuum and dust. With that new information, I stood back and tried to compose myself. The bulge in my pants was obvious, and I caught Katharine staring at it.

"If it's any consolation, I'm soaking wet," she said coyly.

"Don't tell me that, counselor, or the cleaning crew will get quite the surprise."

She was laughing as she gathered her things and we left for dinner. She wanted to go back to my restaurant. She said she needed a good Italian meal to keep her energy up. She teased me that my hearty sexual appetite was exhausting. I teased her right back, because she initiated sex just as much as I did. "Don't put all the blame on me, Katharine. You seem to have a need to make up for your arduous year of abstinence," I reminded her. "Well, if you weren't such a fine specimen," she advised me, "then I wouldn't be so inclined to initiate sex so often. I don't know how any sane woman could resist the masculine pheromones that radiate from your body. I am only human, you know." And with that declaration, we both started to laugh.

I told her how excited Emily was about the opportunity to intern at her firm, and Katharine said she'd found two attorneys looking for interns. Emily needed to be interviewed by each of them the next time she was in town to figure out which one would be a better fit. I told her that Emily would be home for Thanksgiving, and Katharine handed me a slip of paper with their contact information.

Katharine had also spoken to her son Jack about the possible internship with my advertising firm. He knew all about my company, she said, and was excited to talk to someone about the position. I told her I would get her the contact information the following day so that Jack could call and arrange a meeting. It felt good that we were able to help each other out with our childrens' dreams. It felt even better to be able to put a smile on her beautiful face. I had to pinch myself. Where had this woman been all my life?

Dinner was almost ending, and I didn't think I could handle spending the night without her. After the passionate kiss in her office, I was pretty confident she was feeling the same way. We were having an after-dinner drink when I asked her if she wanted to spend the night at my place.

"You want to have a sleepover, Mr. Jensen?" she teased.

"I don't want to sleep much, but yes, I would love to have a sleepover with you," I said with a laugh.

"I'd love it. In fact, I'd love to see where you live."

"I would love to show you where I live. To be honest, I've never brought a woman to my place before," I admitted to her.

"Is that so? Well, I'm honored to be the first woman you take there. Do you mind if we stop by my place so I can grab a few things for work tomorrow and feed the cat?"

"Of course not. Actually, I have a request about what you should pack, if you don't mind. I think you should bring your Yale T-shirt. That's probably my favorite outfit of yours that I've seen you in thus far," I suggested as seriously as I could.

"Consider it packed."

25

*I*an pulled up in front of my apartment and waited for me while I went upstairs to feed Tabby and pack a bag. I couldn't believe that after our wonderful weekend together, I felt nervous about spending the night at his place. I'd asked him if he was serious about never having a woman in his apartment before, and he said he'd never wanted a woman to see where he lived. He felt like his living space was private and would reveal too much about his lifestyle. I was the first woman he'd felt comfortable bringing to his apartment. He realized that I wasn't interested in his money, just him. "This is the first time I felt proud to share my accomplishments with a woman before," he admitted to me. "I've always felt the need to protect myself. There is a part of me that assumes that all the women I go out with have an alterior motive. But with you it's different. I know none of that matters to you. It's refreshing to not be so guarded. I'm not sure how to thank you." Every time Ian opened up to me, I found myself even more intrigued by him. I didn't know how to respond to that, so I just leaned over and kissed him gently.

We didn't get to his place until close to eleven. His driver dropped us off, and we walked into a beautiful foyer hand-in-hand. He used a special key to take us to the top floor. While the elevator ascended, he leaned toward me and kissed my neck. I felt goose bumps run up and down my body.

It was unbelievable how this man affected me. When the door opened, we walked down a short corridor to his unit. He unlocked the door, and I was flabbergasted by the space in front of me. I walked into a large room with cathedral ceilings and large, contemporary furniture filling the space. There was a whole wall of floor-to-ceiling windows overlooking the city. The view was spectacular. The kitchen and dining space were connected to his massive living room, one room flowing into the next. The space was open and elegant, and I loved everything about it. It was such a contrast to my own. I lived in smaller rooms, with smaller windows and cozier furniture. I loved my place, but there was something about the expanse of his apartment that was fascinating. Even his living space was sexy.

He set our briefcases down, grabbed my hand again, and led me into his bedroom. Massive windows overlooking New York lined this room as well, and I couldn't get over the view. He pointed to the bathroom to show me where it was and set my bag on his dresser.

I grabbed my Yale shirt and toothbrush out of my bag and went into the bathroom to change and freshen up. When I came out, he was lying in bed with just his boxer briefs on. The way they sculpted his body was lethal. He told me he had used the other bathroom to brush his teeth, because he didn't want to waste any time. He patted the empty side of the bed, indicating that I should lie down next to him, and put on some soft jazz music. I wasn't sure where it was coming from, but the sound surrounded us beautifully.

We climbed under the covers, and I snuggled next to him. Although his boxers were sexy as hell, they needed to go. I helped him take them off. Oh yes, I much preferred him naked. The sight of his body was all it took to get my engines racing. I tilted my head up and started to kiss him. He put one arm around my back, and his other hand held onto the back of my head so I'd be more comfortable kissing him. It didn't take long for our kissing to become more frantic. The more intense our kissing became, the more our hands wandered. I felt like I needed to explore his body all over again. It was exciting to be in his bed; it made me feel special knowing I was the first woman he'd shared it with. I needed to show him how appreciative I was, so that is exactly what I did.

26

It's hard to predict how your life is going to turn out. I thought I was going to be married to my wife forever. That didn't happen. She tore my heart out when she cheated on me. The only good thing that came out of our marriage was our two beautiful daughters. There was a part of me that couldn't imagine ever bringing another woman to my apartment. I had accepted the fact that I would probably never fall in love again. I didn't think I'd have the nerve to risk opening up my heart again. I didn't want to experience that kind of betrayal from another woman for as long as I lived.

But here was the most incredible woman, lying next to me in my bed. There was no reservation in my mind about my decision. I wanted her here desperately. I'd fantasized about her being here since the first night we met. It was crazy to admit it after such a short time, but I was in love with this woman.

We collapsed in a satiated heap around one in the morning. Our lovemaking was highly energized. I think she liked having sex in new places, and it felt special to have her in my bed, that was for sure. We couldn't keep our hands off one another. Even while we slept, our bodies were intertwined. I slept so much better with her by my side. It had only been a week, but I was confident that I never wanted to sleep alone again. I wanted Katharine—always.

27

I wouldn't have thought it was possible to fall in love after such a short time, but I knew that I had. Maybe since I was older, I was more aware of what I wanted. There was a small part of my brain overanalyzing what was happening with Ian, but I have always been a pretty logical woman. I prayed that I wasn't grasping onto him because I had been so lonely, and he was filling a void. He was so different from Bryce. He was more spontaneous, which I found exciting. He planned a weekend for us, but he had a backup plan in case I wasn't comfortable with the plans he had made. He was thoughtful and resourceful. My husband and I had a fairly rigid routine, because we were both steadfast on finding success in our careers. And even when we found success, our lives were very organized. Both Ian and I had stayed at each other's home without any prior notice or planning. Spontaneity was such an exciting addendum to this relationship. It was very new to me. It was refreshing.

Although Bryce and I had an excellent sex life, this was different. Ian was extremely strong and profoundly fit. Some of the positions we made love in were creative, to say the least. His physical prowess lead to some interesting and satisfying rounds of love making. I'm not sure how I survived the past year without sex, and I didn't want to ever go without it again. I forgot how much I enjoyed being with a man. Ian was a talented and enthusiastic lover. We had an incredible chemistry. We laughed freely. We debated intelligently. I was confident that it wasn't a rebound situation: I had really found passion again. It felt like a miracle.

We fell into a routine where we'd meet for dinner most nights after work and take turns staying at each other's apartments. If one of us had a meeting or needed to get a workout in, we would meet later in the evening, in time for bed. Where we stayed usually depended on the restaurant we went to. We tried to walk home after our meals so we wouldn't be too full when we got home—a full stomach had the potential to interfere with our acrobatic sex life.

I couldn't get over how much sex we had. Our lovemaking was constant. We were insanely attracted to each other and couldn't seem to get our fill. He continued to wow me with his stamina and strength. Sex had been great with my husband, but this was different. It was more than just intense. It was so much fun! I felt like a waif, the way he tossed me around. We often went without sleep in order to satisfy our continued passion, and it wasn't uncommon for one of us to wake up in the middle of the night needing another round. When we would get tired enough, we'd succumb to a few hours of sleep; once we quelled the itch, the adult part of our brains would intercede and demand rest.

About a month into our relationship, he asked me if I'd be able to go to lunch with him and his daughter Sara, the sophomore at Fordham. I was nervous about meeting her. I knew she had a strained relationship with her mother, but I had no idea how she would react to me. I knew it could be hard for some kids to accept their parents dating other people even if the marriage was permanently over. I accepted the invitation with hesitation. Even though I was in love with her dad, that didn't mean she would automatically like me. But it was time to find out one way or the other.

"She's going to love you, Katharine," Ian tried to reassure me. He always seemed to know what I was thinking.

"God, I hope so, because I really love her dad."

We had already exchanged our professions of love to one another. It had happened the second week we were together. We had walked to the National September 11 Memorial after dinner one night. After several minutes of silence, he'd turned to me and brought his face close to mine, holding the sides of my head in his hands. He was gentle, loving and very serious. I wanted to say something, but I didn't want to interrupt whatever he needed to share with me.

"I thank God every day for bringing you into my life. When I think of all the people who died here and how much their families have lost, I don't want to waste a minute. I love you, Katharine Collins. You've brought me more joy in the past month than I've felt in years. I need you to know how much you mean to me. I don't want to scare you, but I have to be honest. I'm in love with you."

I felt tears forming in my eyes as he shared his feelings. He was much more demonstrative than I was used to. It was a little scary, but it was exactly what I was hoping to hear. I felt absolutely the same way, but it took a moment to collect myself before I could respond to him.

"You're not alone with those feelings. I feel exactly the same way. I'm not scared. I love *you*, Ian Jensen. You came into my life at the most perfect time, and I hope you will always remain in my life."

We hugged, and we cried. It was a really special moment that I would forever treasure. I cannot believe I found love a second time. It was almost too much to process. I thought I would spend the rest of my life alone, as a widow. Everything changed when Ian walked into my life. I was so grateful that fate was giving me a second chance. Now I had to believe his daughter would like me, because I knew in my heart of hearts that her dad was my forever.

28

My daughter picked the restaurant where we'd be meeting for lunch. Katharine was planning to meet us there. I decided to walk; it was only fifteen blocks, and I needed to get rid of my nervous energy. I knew Sara would love Katharine—she was amazing. I was just nervous because my daughter was such a spitfire. She always said what she felt; it was impossible for her to hold back. It could be endearing; it could also be annoying as hell. If nothing else, it was genuine and honest. She had always been the more precocious child between my girls, and I knew she would let me know exactly how she felt about my new girlfriend.

Sara arrived at the same time as I did. As usual, she wanted to go for sushi. It was her favorite food, and she liked it when I paid the check; it was an expensive addiction. Katharine hadn't arrived yet, so we got a table, and I sent her a message to tell her we were sitting down. As soon as we sat down and waters were placed in front of us, Katharine approached the table. I jumped out of my seat to greet her. My smile must have been infectious, because she smiled back at me and leaned in for a kiss. We rarely saw each other during the day, so this was a treat. I turned toward my daughter to start the introductions when she said, "Jeez, you guys got it bad! Get a room already."

Katharine laughed and reached out to shake Sara's hand. "It's a pleasure to finally meet you. And yes, I can only speak for myself, but I've got it *real* bad."

"That makes two of us," I had to add.

The lunch went better than I could have imagined. The girls chatted happily—I didn't even need to be there. Sara noticed Katharine's designer shoes, and they had a conversation about fashion that I thought would never end. Katharine told Sara that she had a friend in Paris who was able to get her designer clothes, shoes, and purses at a wholesale price. She offered to show Sara the items that were available for purchase the next time she got an e-mail from her friend. Sara was ecstatic.

Katharine asked her about her classes and what her plans were for the future. She told Katharine she didn't want to be a boring attorney like her sister. I cleared my throat, and Sara burst out laughing then apologized profusely.

"That's OK, Sara. Most attorneys are pretty boring," Katharine said kindly. It was obvious she was amused by my daughter's candor. Although my daughter was bright, her personality was quirky and often flippant. I loved her familiar and easy-going demeanor, but it took some people a little time to warm up to her. I was happy to see that Katharine wasn't offended by my daughter's behavior and was, in fact, enjoying their exchange.

"I didn't mean to insult you, Katharine. You don't seem boring at all. In fact, you're way cooler than I thought you'd be. As for school, I was thinking about medicine, but my physiology class is kicking my ass. Now I'm not sure if I want to stick with it or not. Who knows? I'm not worried about it though. I'll figure something out. I always do. OK, enough about school. I want to know more about you and your family. So what's your son like?"

Sara had a ton of questions about Jack. The more Katharine talked about him, the more fascinated Sara seemed. She had told me the other day that she had broken up with her boyfriend because he was lame and never wanted to do anything but play video games. She kept insisting she would be more fun to play with than the remote control, but he didn't get the hint. It was more than I needed to know, but I loved the fact that she was passionate and honest. I was so proud of my little girl.

"So, Katharine, when do I get to meet this dreamy-sounding son of yours?"

"I was thinking, if it's all right with your father, that I would love to have all three of our children join us for Thanksgiving at my place," Katharine suggested.

"Dad, what do you think? I think it'd be great. I know Em is dying to meet Katharine, too. And then I can find out more about Jackson. We usually go out to dinner on Thanksgiving, and it just isn't the same. I'd love a home-cooked meal. What do you say, Dad?" Sara asked enthusiastically.

"There's no place I'd rather be. Will Jack be comfortable with us being there?" I asked her carefully.

"I already asked him if it was OK if I invited your family over, and he said it would be nice to have a good Thanksgiving memory since last year 'sucked huge'—as he put it."

We all laughed. The rest of the lunch went by too quickly. Sara had a class she needed to get to, and Katharine had a meeting. I stood up and hugged both of my girls. I added an incredibly sensual kiss on Katharine's lips, then whispered in her ear—something naughty that I was sure my daughter couldn't hear. Katharine laughed wholeheartedly, said good-bye to Sara, and was off. Sara stayed behind. I knew she had something to say to me.

"She's amazing, Dad! I'm so happy you found her. Now don't do anything to screw this up, you hear me?" she said firmly.

I enveloped her in a huge hug. I told her I loved her, and I promised I wasn't going to screw things up. I loved Katharine, and we were very happy.

29

Before I knew it, Thanksgiving week was here. I took the day before off and closed my office Thursday and Friday so my staff could enjoy a long weekend. Jack was due home Wednesday afternoon, and I couldn't wait to see him. I ordered Thai food to be delivered for lunch as I prepared some of the meal for the next day. He came bouncing into the apartment at 1:30 p.m., and we sat at the kitchen counter eating and catching up. After an hour, he left to hang out with some friends, and we agreed to meet for dinner. He picked the restaurant, and I told him I would call for reservations and text him the time.

He never mentioned Ian's name, so I didn't bring it up. He knew we were having him and his two girls for dinner the next day, and he said he was OK with it. I just prayed he'd give Ian a chance. I had to believe they would like each other. If they didn't, I didn't know what I would do. Although I loved my son desperately, I loved Ian too. I'd hate to be forced to choose between them. This was turning out to be more stressful than I'd imagined.

As if reading my mind, Ian called me.

"Hey, counselor, miss me?"

"More than you know. Jack just left to hang out with friends, and I'm not going to lie—I'm freaking out about tomorrow."

"It's going to be great. I think Jack will see that I love you—and I plan on loving you for a long time. I had a feeling you were stressing. How about I stop by for a quickie?" he suggested with the sexiest laugh.

"I don't think that's a good idea—what if Jack comes home early? Can I have a rain check?" I asked sweetly.

"That's a silly question, Katharine. I love you, and I'll see you tomorrow."

I spent the rest of the afternoon making Thanksgiving dinner. I didn't know why anyone thought all this preparation was worth it: it would take about eight hours to prepare the meal, and about twenty minutes to consume it. I was excited about bringing our two families together, but this kind of food prep seemed a little extreme. I'd have to rethink my offer to make Thanksgiving dinner next year. *Next year*. God, it was good to be thinking about the future again.

I met my son at his favorite restaurant around eight o'clock. Dinner was great. Jack wanted to talk about Bryce a lot, and it felt good being able to talk about him without sobbing. We were able to share happy memories, which felt amazing. We also talked about how difficult things had been since he died. Jack told me that he had been seeing a therapist, and I was glad to hear it. "So when did you start seeing this Dr. Wells?" I asked him.

"Pretty much when school started. I felt really guilty leaving you, but I knew both you and dad were excited about me going to Yale and I wanted to make you proud. I just worried about you constantly, and I was so sad about dad dying. I figured I would try the whole counseling thing out, as long as she didn't want me to take meds. I was sad, but I wasn't depressed. She has been really great. I'm glad I found her."

I was surprised he hadn't told me about it sooner, but he said he hadn't wanted to worry me since I was having such a hard time myself. I told him that I had stopped going to therapy at the end of the summer. He wanted to know if Ian was the reason. I had to be honest with him. "Ian was definitely a part of it. Honestly, I was tired of sitting in the therapist's office crying every week. I didn't feel like I was making any headway. Sleeping and eating were still a chore for me. She actually suggested medication, but I refused to consider it. I was hoping the sessions would make me feel better and give me coping strategies, but they didn't. Therapy hadn't made me feel better at all. It was exhausting and draining, and it made me very sad. No matter how much I loved your father, nothing I did could bring him back. It sucked, but those were the cards we were dealt. I actually stopped seeing the therapist a few months before I met Ian. Once I met Ian, I realized that being in a relationship was the best medicine ever."

"I've missed talking to you mom. I have been afraid to upset you. It feels good to be able to talk to you openly again," he confided to me. "And I'm looking forward to meeting Ian. If you think he's a great guy, then he must be."

"He is very special, and it is very important to me that you like him. But no matter how you feel about him, you need to be honest with me. Promise?"

"Of course. I may have kept the therapy thing from you, but I would never lie to you," he reassured me.

I admitted to Jack that I was ready to move on. It was difficult to say the words out loud to him, but he needed to know how serious I was about Ian. I also told my son that I would never forget his father or stop loving him. He needed to hear that as well. I reminded Jack that I loved Bryce with every fiber of my being, and that if he hadn't died, we would still be happily and lovingly together. I prayed that one day, he would find the kind of love his father and I had shared. We had been so blessed. It had been an incredible love story. But it was over, and I'd promised his dad that I would move on.

At this point, I did start to cry. My son could see how difficult this conversation was for me, but he had more questions, and I knew that I needed to answer each and every one of them. Jack wanted to know what I meant about promising Bryce I'd move on. I had never told Jack about our pact, or about the two-pimento signal we'd agreed on. He was an adult now, however, and I knew he could handle it. If he was interested in knowing more, then I had to be forthcoming with him.

Jack sat quietly through my story. When I finished, he reached over and took my hand in his. He thanked me for being honest—even though it was awkward to hear. He was floored by the two pimentos in the olive story and agreed with me that it was pretty freaky. I told him that I still had the olive in the freezer back at our apartment. He asked me if he could see it, and I told him I would be happy to show it to him, since I truly believed it was a sign from his dad.

"I can't believe you guys made that kind of promise to one another," he admitted after I had finished with every detail from the story.

"I know it sounds crazy, but it's the truth. Your dad and I had something incredibly special. Our love was so strong that the thought of the other person living the rest of their life alone was excrutiating. It is incredible how selfless you can be when you love someone. And I loved your dad with all my heart. I always will Jackson. You need to remember that."

The rest of the dinner was more upbeat. It felt like we had survived an intense therapy session and now felt free to move forward. We'd said what we needed to say, and I was glad that it was over. Now it was time to introduce the two men in my life to one another and see what happened.

30

I hadn't expected my mom to fall in love so quickly after Dad died. The rational part of my brain understood that she was young and beautiful and shouldn't have to spend the rest of her life alone. The other part of me resented another man in her life, no matter who he was. I'm glad we had the conversation last night, but I was still freaking out a little. I promised myself I would give this guy a chance. I had to. I loved my mom, and I didn't want her to be sad anymore. She really did look better. It was so good to see her smile and laugh again. At one point she had looked so unhappy and so thin that I was scared she was going to die, too. If Ian was the one that made her want to keep on living, I had to give him the chance.

I had told my therapist that my mom was seeing another man. After she let me vent for a while, she told me that what I was feeling was normal, but she asked if I really thought Mom, a forty-six-year-old woman, should spend the rest of her life alone. I realized that wouldn't bring my dad back; nothing would. I needed to be open-minded and supportive. So here it was. I was going to come face-to-face with this Ian guy. And, to make matters worse, his two daughters.

Thanksgiving morning arrived sooner than I had hoped. I woke up to the smell of food cooking and looked at the clock. It was nine in the morning—only three more hours until the big introduction. I was a mess. I went to the kitchen, gave Mom a kiss, and told her I was going for a run. I loved running through the city. There was always something going on no matter what time of the day or night it was. I was hoping that some exercise would clear my head.

I ran hard for over an hour and realized that I should get back to the apartment to help with the preparations. When I got back to our place, I grabbed a bottle of water out of the fridge and told mom that I was going to take a quick shower and then help her out. She gave me a big smile, but it seemed a little forced. I think she was nervous as well.

At noon, the doorman told us that the Jensen family had arrived. I told him to send them up. I told Mom that I would let them in, since she was in the middle of doing something messy with the turkey. When I opened the door, I couldn't help but smile. This guy had some good-looking daughters. Holy crap. I hadn't thought to ask how old his daughters were; I'd just assumed they were young and annoying. One of the girls had straight brown hair, was very thin, and was dressed rather conservatively in a black pantsuit. She may have been plainly dressed, but she looked like a model. The other girl had wavy blond hair, the most piercing blue eyes I had ever seen, and an hourglass figure that was so sexy I think my mouth fell open. I couldn't help but stare at her just a bit longer. She was dressed in a bright turquoise dress that made her eyes sparkle even more. After my moment of gawking had subsided, I reached out my hand and introduced myself to Ian and his daughters. Once the pleasantries had finished, I escorted them to the kitchen.

Ian walked over and kissed my mom on the cheek. As soon as my mom finished greeting Ian, she walked over to the adorable blonde and gave her a big hug. It was obvious that they had met before. She looked at the brunette next and shook her hand and told her it was nice to finally meet her. The girl gave her such a sweet smile that I knew my mom would reach out and hug her. And she did. The girl was receptive to my mom's embrace, which made me feel good. OK, maybe this wouldn't be so bad after all.

Ian had brought flowers and wine. My mom put the flowers in a vase, and I proceeded to open the wine. Once we all had a glass, we toasted to the holiday and began to nibble on appetizers. I learned that the conservative girl, Emily, was interning at my mom's firm this summer and going to law school in the fall. She was actually really nice and seemed genuinely grateful for my mom's help in securing the internship. The blue-eyed goddess was named Sara. She was a ball of energy. She was a sophomore at Fordham and didn't know what she wanted to do yet. Her grades were good, but she told us she was focusing on enjoying the college experience before life got too serious. It sounded like she was partying a lot and was involved in a ton of fun social clubs. I liked her a lot. She kept all of us laughing.

I found out that Emily was dating a guy who was off to medical school in the fall. Her face softened when she spoke of him. They had been dating for almost two years. If he got into medical school in the same city, the plan was for them to live together. My mother told Emily that my dad had chosen Yale for graduate school so he could be with her. I was surprised that she mentioned my dad, but it wasn't awkward at all. I watched Ian's face, and he seemed totally cool when she talked about him. I was starting to like this guy.

Sara boasted about being single. She told us about dumping the video-playing boyfriend and said that she was having way too much fun to be saddled down in some "ho-hum relationship." Her expressions were as cute as she was. We were in the same year at college, so we had a lot to talk about. The three of us monopolized the conversation the first hour, which seemed to please our parents considerably. This was going so much better than I ever thought possible. The only awkward thing was that I pretty attracted to Sara, and I wondered to myself, if it was obvious.

31

I couldn't believe how gracious Katharine's son was. He seemed genuinely interested in my daughters, which made me so happy. The way the three of them laughed and carried on made it seem like they had been friends forever. They had a lot of things in common and even teased each other from time to time. At one point, Katharine reached for my hand and gave me a wink. I knew what she was thinking. She was feeling as grateful as I was. Our kids liked each other.

Dinner was excellent. I wasn't expecting Katharine to be such a good cook. Since we always went out to dinner, I assumed that her skills weren't that strong in the kitchen. She proved me wrong. It was the most gourmet thanksgiving dinner I had ever had. I wondered what other talents she was hiding from me. I looked forward to finding out.

The five of us went through three bottles of wine, and the conversation and laughter continued through to dessert. There was no awkwardness, even when Sara mentioned Jack's dad dying. She said that she felt sad for him, because she would be devastated if anything ever happened to me. He thanked her and said that, although it had been a really tough year, he and his mom were figuring out how to move on. After he said that, Jack looked at me and thanked me for being a part of his mom's life. It was a sentimental and honest moment. I assured him that I wasn't trying to take Bryce's place, but I did want to be a part of Katharine's life. Jack seemed at ease with this. He leaned over and shook my hand and then kissed his mom on the cheek. That was when I noticed that she was crying. It was a special moment. I felt very thankful.

Sara made sure the sappy exchange didn't carry on indefinitely. She told everybody to snap out of it and help the amazing cook clean up the meal. We all worked together and cleaned up the kitchen in record time. Emily thanked the hostess profusely and excused herself to meet up with Martin's family for a few hours. Sara and Jack had wandered into the living room, where it sounded like they were making plans. I asked them what was going on, and they told me they had decided to go to some horror flick that had opened the week before. It appeared that horror films were another common interest of theirs. The last matinee was at 5:30 p.m., so they were off to the movies.

The last thing I had expected was that the day would go so smoothly. Even more surprising was how well Sara and Jack got along. I couldn't believe they were going to the movies together. It was a wonderfully unexpected turn of events—and it also meant that Katharine and I would have some time alone.

32

It was a spectacular Thanksgiving celebration, and before I knew it, Ian and I were alone. I was thrilled. I felt like a nervous teenager who suddenly had the house to herself with no parents lurking around. More importantly, I felt like we had something momentous to celebrate. Thanksgiving had been a huge success. We knew we would have about three hours alone before Jack and Sara returned from the movies, and we weren't going to waste one minute.

"First one naked gets to decide the first position!" Ian yelled joyfully as he ran toward my bedroom. Fortunately, I had a dress on and was able to remove it while I was running. I was also able to unhook my bra and slip out of my panties before he was able to get his socks off. Naturally, I won. Of course, we would both win in the end, but I loved his playful attitude. When he finally got his socks off, I pushed him onto the bed so I could stare at his naked body.

"What shall I do with you?" I asked seductively.

"I'm at your mercy," he conceded.

"Let's see how much my little friend here wants me," I said, staring as his growing appendage.

Since we had a fair amount of time, I decided to make him suffer. I started at the end of the bed first. I sucked his toes and massaged his feet.

When I finally looked up, his eyes were closed, and he was getting huge. I crawled upward and massaged the inside of his thighs, careful not to touch him where he wanted me to. I needed to make him squirm for a bit. I skipped his midsection and found his nipples. I sucked on them until they grew hard, and he moaned, begging me to touch him somewhere else. I hushed him and continued my assault. I sucked on his neck and his ears. He started to grab for me, but I pushed his hands above his head. I ended my travels at his mouth. I sucked on his lips and found his tongue, kissing him with the same intensity I could feel pulsating between his legs. When his begging got pathetic and I knew I couldn't take any more, I straddled his thighs.

"This is the position I choose, Mr. Jensen."

I lowered my dripping midsection onto his hard, throbbing body. I was wet and tight, and I knew it had to feel as delicious for him as it did for me. Once I had him nestled inside of me, I started to ride him—up and down, up and down. He started to moan, and I stifled him with my mouth. As the tension built, our tempo increased. I loved riding him. The orgasms were so intense this way. I loved the way I could control my release so it coincided with his, and that is exactly what happened. We came together in a moment of indescribable satisfaction.

The connection felt even stronger this time. Maybe it was due to the fact that our kids genuinely liked each other. That had to be a big part of it. It could also have been the release we needed after worrying about this day. Either way, it was magical. I felt my orgasm throughout my entire body.

After I slid off his body and curled up in his arms, I fell sound asleep. Food, wine, and satisfying sex were all I needed to fully relax.

33

I didn't want to wake Katharine, but I didn't want the kids to find us in bed together, either. I snuck out of the bed as quietly as possible, went into the bathroom, and got dressed again. I went into the living room, lit the fire, and sat down to read.

Around eight o'clock, I heard the laughter in the foyer. Jack and Sara were debating what the scariest part of the movie had been; their camaraderie made me so happy. After they walked into the kitchen and grabbed some water bottles from the fridge, they noticed me sitting by the fire.

"Hey, Dad. What's going on? Where's Katharine?" Sara asked.

"She excused herself and went to bed about an hour ago. Thanksgiving knocked her out," I explained to them.

"Mom was pretty nerved out about today. I hope she felt good about how it turned out," Jack said.

"She was thrilled that you kids got along so well," I offered.

"Your daughters are great, Ian. I'm glad you guys could spend the holiday with us. It was important that mom and I made a new memory. Last year sucked so bad."

"It was our pleasure, Jack. Thank you again for allowing us to join you on this special day. I think I'm going to say good night to your mom and head home."

"Sounds good. Sara and I are going to hang out for a little while, if that's OK with you."

"That's fine. Have a good evening. Just call for the car when you're ready to come home, Sara," I reminded her.

"Will do. Later, gator!" Sara said as she kissed me.

I snuck into Katharine's bedroom and couldn't believe how peaceful she looked. I didn't have the heart to wake her, so I found a notepad next to her bed and left her a note.

> *Dear Katharine,*
>
> *Today was very special. I am so thankful that you came into my life. I'll miss you tonight. Dream happy, my love. I'll see you in the morning.*
>
> *Love, Ian*

34

I woke up slightly confused. Sun was streaming in the windows. Was it morning already and where had Ian gone? I looked at the clock. It was almost seven. I couldn't believe it. I hadn't slept that long in ages. I was stretching and thinking about Thanksgiving when I noticed a note on the pillow next to me.

I read the note from Ian and couldn't help but smile. He was so wonderful, and Jack liked him. I hadn't realized how important that was to me. My guys liked each other. It brought me so much joy.

Sometimes I felt a little guilty about finding happiness again. It was a strange sensation, but every once in a while it was exactly how I felt. Part of me felt as though, despite our pact, I was betraying the memory of my husband by moving on. I had been walking around in such a dismal funk for so long that it felt so strange to have good feelings on a daily basis again. I closed my eyes and said a quiet prayer. I needed some kind of reassurance that I was doing the right thing. As I prayed for guidance, the image of the olive kept invading my thoughts. It made me smile. Bryce didn't want me to be sad anymore. Frankly, neither did I.

I opened my eyes and stared out the window at the beautiful day. This waking up alone nonsense was for the birds. I felt lonely in my bed and thought about texting Ian, but I didn't want to wake him. I jumped in the shower and shaved my legs. When I got out, I decided to put on a little makeup and dry my hair. As I was brushing my teeth, I heard a knock on my bathroom door.

"I wanted to serve you coffee in bed, but you weren't there. Why are you up so early, counselor?" I heard Ian say.

I rinsed my mouth, opened the door, and pulled him into the most scandalous kiss. He responded with such fervor that I could feel my arousal growing. It didn't help that I was only in my undies and his favorite Yale shirt.

"We better cool it. I'd hate for Jack to hear us," I said.

"I bring good news. Jack was in the kitchen when I got here. He wanted me to tell you he was going over to Tommy's for breakfast then to the club to play squash. He said he'd be back to for lunch around noon. It's just you and me and a strong cup of coffee and cream, my lady."

"Then let me crawl back to bed and you can bring me my coffee. I'm up for a do-over this morning," I teased him.

By the time we'd finished fooling around, the coffee was cold. It didn't matter. Sex with Ian was a better way to wake up than coffee ever could be. Having two orgasms before eight in the morning was a perfect way to start the day.

We talked about our plans for the rest of the day. Ian was taking his girls to see his parents in the afternoon, and they were planning on having dinner there. Jack had said he wanted to lie low with me. We planned on ordering some kind of takeout and watching a movie together.

"How would you feel about the five of us getting together again?" I asked. "I don't want to rush things, but yesterday was such a great time. Maybe you could see if the girls are interested in going out to dinner tomorrow night. We could even go to a show beforehand."

Ian smiled. "Sounds like a great plan. I think it would be awesome for all of us to get together again, especially if you don't have to cook all day to make it happen. But I have to say—I have one problem with our plans for the weekend."

"What problem?" I asked.

"I don't get to have a sleepover with my favorite girl for two more nights. I hated waking up alone this morning. I can't sleep without you next to me. Solitary slumber is very detrimental to my health," he whined.

"I missed you, too, but we've managed to sleep apart for nearly fifty years. I don't think two more nights will ignite some fatal disease in your body."

"I suppose you're right. Doesn't mean I'm going to like it, though. I think these are going to be the longest two nights of my life." He leaned over and kissed me hard.

35

oly crap, what was wrong with me? There were so many women at Yale to choose from and here I was, smitten with my mom's boyfriend's daughter. I couldn't help it, though. She was so freaking adorable. We'd had so much fun last night. During the movie, she'd gotten so scared that she'd practically jumped in my lap and buried her head in my chest. She felt amazing to hold. I wrapped my arms around her and tried to protect her from the horrifying images on the movie screen. I had never felt so comfortable holding a girl before. I could have held onto her forever.

Her body was warm and soft, and she wore a musky perfume that reeked of sex. OK, maybe that wasn't the best description, but sex was all I could think of when I smelled her. I could feel myself getting hard as I held her, and I prayed to God she wouldn't notice. A guy's body can betray him in an instant, and it totally sucks. I didn't want to embarrass myself or make her feel uncomfortable, but I had no control of how hard I got. I wrapped my arms around her and whispered random things in her ears to calm her down while one particularly gruesome scene played out. When it was over, she sat back in her seat and grabbed my hand.

"Thanks for that," she said.

"My pleasure. The scene was a little over the top, even for me," I admitted.

"I'm usually not such a wuss, but the way he was gouging out her eyes made me want to throw up that beautiful dinner your mom made."

"Where did you meet my mom before? It seemed like you guys had already met," I asked.

"Oh yeah, we had lunch together about a week ago. Your mom is so cool. I'm kind of jealous—my mom's a total flake. My sister and I decided to live with Dad after they split, because Mom got more whacked out every day. Besides, we never spent any time with her when we all lived together; we always had nannies and babysitters. Sometimes, the cleaning ladies would watch us so she could go do her own thing—shopping, going out with friends, partying...She was never a very good mom. It sucked, but I'm over it now."

"I'm really sorry. I knew they got a divorce, but I didn't know the details. Jeez, it sounds like she didn't even want to be a mom. That totally sucks. How's your relationship with her now?"

"Not great. She cheated on my dad, and now she's living with the guy she was screwing. He's a trainer at her gym. He's good-looking and stuff, but it's still weird—he's so much younger than she is. I doubt he makes much money, and my dad's stupid rich, so Mom tried to get a ridiculous settlement. It didn't work though. She gets a monthly allowance, but she's not happy with it."

"If it's any consolation, my mom is one of the most loyal people you could ever meet. She was so devoted to my dad; she was so devastated when he died that I was scared she was going to die, too. It's been the shittiest year ever. I'm so glad she met your dad. She really likes him. And you don't have to worry about her wanting his money. She's got plenty of her own, and besides, she isn't like that," I shared.

"My dad's really happy with her, too. You should hear how he talks about her. It's adorable. He couldn't wait for us to meet her. I was really surprised—after what my mom did, my dad swore off women. He kept saying that Em and I were the only women he needed in his life. I knew that was bullshit, but he'd been saying it for years. All he did was work and exercise. We prayed he'd find somebody nice, and *voila*—there came your mom!" Sara beamed.

"Thanks, Sara. That means a lot to me. All of this turned out so much better than I thought it would. I'm stoked that your dad is so nice, and you guys are so cool."

When the movie ended, I wasn't ready for our time to be over. We had a lot of things to talk about. Sara was different than other girls. I loved her constant chatter and energy. It was obvious that the divorce had forced her to grow up; it seemed like she had a really good perspective on things. I didn't even care she was Ian's daughter—I liked her. I invited her back to our apartment, which she gladly agreed to. I got the feeling she liked me just as much as I liked her. It was strange, but cool.

We watched *Cast Away* with Tom Hanks and ate some popcorn in our living room. When he lost his volleyball, we both got choked up. If you have any human emotion, it's impossible not to feel Tom Hank's pain when he loses Wilson. As we were sitting there in silence, tears in our eyes, we looked at each other and burst into hysterical laughter. Crying over a volleyball seems absurd, but it's a tough scene to watch; it gets to me every time. It obviously affected Sara the same way. When it was time for her to go back to her dad's, I offered to walk her home. It was about a twenty-minute walk, but it was pretty nice out, and I was hoping to get a little more time with her. We chatted the whole way to her dad's. We had a ton in common, and I loved being with her. I wasn't sure what to do before I left her, so I gave her a hug and thanked her for a great night.

She hugged me back. "I'm glad Katharine has such a cool son," she said playfully.

"And I'm glad Ian has such a cool daughter," I said earnestly.

"See ya later, Wilson," she joked.

"Later," I replied with a laugh.

She smiled, stood up on her toes, and kissed my cheek. Then she ran up the stairs to the entrance of her building. I was elated. I had to find a way to see her again.

36

After we had our coffee in bed, Ian left before Jack got home from his friend's. I wanted some time with my son, and I didn't want him to think Ian had totally invaded our lives. Jack said he felt like sushi, so we walked to our favorite Japanese restaurant. I was anxious to hear what he'd thought about Thanksgiving, but I waited until we ordered before I asked him.

"What did you think of the Jensens?" I asked cautiously.

"Ian is great, Mom. We had a long talk this morning. He's really into you. I'm good with that. Sara told me more about her parents' divorce. His wife sounds like a total bitch. I couldn't even imagine you or Dad cheating," he said reflectively. "I don't know how you could do that to someone you supposedly love. It's such a shitty thing to do."

"I don't believe in cheating. I was completely devoted to your dad, as he was to me. It's the only way to have a relationship, in my opinion. People who cheat are weak and cowardly. I could never be with someone like that. I'm very sad for Ian and the girls—he would have stayed with her; he believed in the vows he took."

"That had to really suck for him. I'm glad he got out. I can't imagine you not wanting to be a part of my life. It would have devastated me. Sara seems to be taking it all in stride, though."

"It sounds like you and Sara spent a lot of time talking," I commented.

"She's pretty great, Mom. It feels kind of weird since she's Ian's kid, but I really like her. We had a blast last night. I don't think I've ever had such a good time with a girl before," he admitted to me hesitantly.

"That's great, Jack. So what if she's Ian's daughter? Friendship—or even love—doesn't care who her dad is or isn't dating. If you like her, then go for it. You should never take being happy for granted: we learned that the hard way, didn't we? If nothing else, you guys sound like you're going to be friends," I told him.

My son looked extremely relieved by what I had said to him. "Really? You don't mind? That's great. I couldn't believe how much I liked her. She is so different than any other girl I've ever gone out with," Jack said in a very relieved tone. "I thought you might be mad—or maybe it would be too weird."

"I'd never be mad if you followed your heart...So, I guess you won't mind if I arrange for the five of us to have dinner Saturday night?"

"That'd be awesome, Mom," Jack said with a grin, "I'd like to spend more time with all three of them. And if he's going to be a part of your life, I need to get to know him better."

37

The girls and I had planned to see my parents on Friday. Emily and Sara hadn't seen their grandparents since the beginning of the semester, and my parents were a huge part of the girls' life. When my wife and I split, they came to the city to help out, taking the girls for a weekend now and again so they could do fun things like sailing and horseback riding. I'm not sure I could have survived without their help.

The ride to my folks' place took about an hour. The traffic was pretty light for a Friday afternoon, and I imagined everyone was taking advantage of the Black Friday sales going on in the city. The girls talked most of the way; it was obvious they'd missed each other as much as I'd missed them. I was so glad that the divorce hadn't pulled the three of us apart. Even though my wife had screwed me, I wasn't about to let her screw with the relationship I had with my daughters. They meant the world to me. And now, so did Katharine.

When I was able to get a word in edgewise, I asked the girls about dinner on Saturday night. Emily had already committed to going to Martin's, but Sara enthusiastically agreed to join us. She wanted to know where we were going and if Jack was going to be there. I was tempted to ask her why she sounded so excited about seeing Jack again, but I didn't want to embarrass her in front of her sister. It sounded to me like she was digging Katharine's son. Well, wasn't that unexpected!

At one point during the drive, I pulled over to talk to them about something serious. They were nervous at first when I told them we needed to talk about something privately as a family, but the conversation went better than I'd expected. They were very receptive to the plan I was formulating. Life had really changed for me, and I felt so blessed that my daughters were supportive. I was so proud of the young women they had become.

My parents were thrilled to see us. They were the healthiest seventy-year-old people you could ever meet. They played golf and tennis. They loved sailing and riding horses. They had a ton of friends and socialized several times a week. Mom had made us her version of a Thanksgiving dinner. It was beautifully presented and scrumptious as ever. It was also much different from Katharine's, so it didn't feel like we were eating the same meal two days in a row.

As dinner was ending, my mother asked me what we had done for Thanksgiving. I was about to answer when Sara chirped in.

"We went to Katharine's, Grandma. That's dad's new girlfriend. She's amazing. You're going to love her!" Sara beamed.

"I've actually met her, sweetheart. Your dad brought her to our B52 benefit last month. She was quite lovely. I'm happy to hear you're still dating her, Ian. Is it serious?"

"Of course it is, Grandma," Sara blurted out. "They're adorable together!"

"Yes, Mom, it's serious," I interrupted my highly enthusiastic daughter. "I love Katharine."

"Love? Are you sure, Ian? You loved the other one—no offense, girls—and she crushed your heart and your bank account. You need to be careful," my mom said possessively.

"Don't worry. She's nothing like their mother. She's an extremely hardworking woman who doesn't want anything from me but love. And I'm confident that she has plenty of her own money and couldn't care less about mine. She's not like that. I think she's my forever, Mom."

"Oh, goodness gracious, that's wonderful!" my mom shouted. She jumped out of her chair and came over to hug me. My dad just smiled my way and said nothing. Both of the girls had big smiles on their faces. I knew they were happy with my decision. It had felt amazing to tell Katharine that I loved her. Now I had said it aloud to the four most important people in my life—and that felt amazing, too. Katharine was my forever. And it was time for her to know that simple and monumental fact.

38

I'm not sure why, but I was nervous about dinner. Jack had confided a pretty serious secret to me when he told me about his attraction to Sara, and I didn't want to share that with Ian until my son gave me permission. I knew it would be hard not analyzing the way Jack and Sara talked and acted around each other, and I was worried that Sara wouldn't be as into Jack as he was into her. You never want to see your children put in an awkward situation—or, even worse, in any kind of pain. I hoped she reciprocated his feelings.

We met at Pane Vino at seven; Sara wanted to see her uncle before she went back to school, and she said she was craving his lasagna and a homemade cannoli. I loved how close their family was, and I knew Jack would love the food. The restaurant held great memories for me since it was the first place Ian ever took me for dinner. Even though I was nervous when we went to the restaurant, as soon as I saw Ian, all my anxiety went away.

Ian and Jack shook hands while Sara and I hugged. When Ian pulled me into an embrace and kissed my cheek, I saw my son give Sara a hug. Ian looked surprised. I was simply happy that Sara returned the gesture with the same intensity. Young love was in front of us. I could feel it.

When Ian looked at me quizzically, I whispered in his ear, "I'll tell you more later."

Dinner was fantastic as usual. Todd came and sat with us for a while. He seemed like a really nice guy. He recognized that I had put on some weight since he'd first met me and jokingly accused Ian of trying to fatten me up so no other men would look at me. Ian yelled at him for being rude, but I knew I wasn't overweight; I took it as a compliment. I knew I looked better. I found out that Todd had been married for about twenty years and had two teenage sons. During the school holidays, they worked at the restaurant, so I was bound to meet them. They went to a private school that Ian paid for. Ian had never mentioned that fact, but it was obvious that his brother was grateful. It was also obvious that my boyfriend was a very generous man with an even more generous heart.

Todd said that he had spoken to their mother that morning, and she was full of news that she couldn't wait to share with the world. He then looked at Ian and asked his big brother if there was anything he wanted to tell him. Ian got a funny look on his face, and Sara giggled. I looked around the table and wondered what I was missing. I stared at Ian until he was forced to meet my gaze.

"What's going on here?" I asked.

"Nothing, really. Uh, the girls told our parents all about Thanksgiving. You know, they talked about us. Sara told my mom all about you. The girls are excited about our relationship. That's all," Ian stammered.

"That's total crap, and you know it, Dad," Sara chimed in.

"Yeah, bro, that's not what mom was telling me," Todd added.

"Ok, Jensen. Fess up. What's going on?" I insisted.

"Can we speak in private, Katharine?" Ian pleaded.

The three spectators at the table all said no—in unison. Now I had to know what was going on. What was the big secret everyone knew except me?

"Fine, I'll indulge you voyeurs. You might as well know what you're in for."

Ian got out of his chair and stood next to me. He took my hand and knelt down on one knee. My mind was racing. What the hell was he doing? There was no way he was going to propose to me—right? We'd just met, for God's sake. We were grown, rational adults. We never discussed marriage. Holy shit, he *was* going to propose to me. What the hell was I going to say?

"Katharine, I never thought I would find love again. I had given up on ever finding someone I would want to spend the rest of my life with, and then you came into my world. You epitomize everything a man could want in a woman. You are brilliant and beautiful, compassionate and funny, loyal and loving. I received permission this morning from the amazing young man you raised. I also received my girls' blessing to follow through with my plan. I wouldn't be doing this unless everyone was on board. And everyone is."

He paused, took a black velvet box from his pocket, and handed it to me. I opened it, and a beautiful sapphire ring glimmered up at me. "This was my grandmother's ring," he continued. "She was one of the most important women in my life. This ring is the only thing I ever want to be blue on you again. Please, Katharine, will you be my forever?"

His forever? I was dumbstruck, utterly speechless. There were no words. His declaration of love was so sincere, and so beautiful, that I couldn't stop the flow of tears. I loved this man. I wanted to be his forever. I just couldn't speak.

"Are you kidding, Mom? Now you're speechless? Would you like me to answer for you?" Jack said in a mocking tone. Although everyone laughed, I couldn't make sense of what was happening.

"Of course I want to be your forever, Ian. I already feel like I am," I whispered. "I never thought I'd fall in love again, and I do love you. I can't believe I found this kind of love again. I have felt so blessed to be given another chance. But it's so soon. And I'm scared. I couldn't bear to lose another man. When Bryce died, a part of me died, too. His death was too painful. I'm so afraid. I don't ever want to go through that again," I confessed.

"I promise to be here for as long as humanly possible. There is no place I'd rather be than by your side. We'll both die one day—it's inevitable. Don't let that ruin what we have now: focus on the love we share. I want to spend the rest of my days with you. Please tell me you want the same thing," he said pleadingly.

I stuck my hand out, indicating that I wanted him to put the ring on my finger. He looked up at me and smiled. Tears were pooling in his eyes. He put the ring on and just held my hand. It fit perfectly. I held his face and gave him a gentle kiss. Then I wrapped my arms around him and starting crying even harder. I noticed Sara getting up and walking toward us. Ian and I stood up to greet her. She hugged us both and was crying as hard as I was. Jack and Todd joined the group hug, and Emily and Martin came into the room just as we relaxed our embrace.

"What are you doing here?" I asked them. "I thought you had other plans."

"Rumor had it there was going to be a proposal tonight. We're sorry we were late. The cab ride took forever. It looks like a congratulations is in order?" Emily asked even though the answer was obvious.

"Yes, baby. She said yes!" Ian told his daughter. Emily walked over to her dad and hugged him hard.

"I thought you were going to wait until after dinner," Emily said.

"Your sister and Uncle Todd couldn't keep a secret, so I was forced to ask her before they did," Ian said as he started to laugh.

"Em, you missed it. Dad got down on his knees and said the mushiest stuff. But don't worry—I recorded the whole thing on my phone," Sara told her.

"And you said yes, Katharine?" Emily asked me again.

"Of course I did. I love your father more than I thought possible. And I promise you, both of you girls, that I don't want anything from your father but his love. I don't need his money, and I don't want it. I also promise I will always be faithful to him. Your father has truly been my knight in shining armor. I want to be his forever, too."

I took Ian's hands in mine, looked him in the eyes, and said, "Ian Jensen, I accept your proposal willingly and without an ounce of hesitation. I want to be yours, forever and ever."

Emily hugged me tightly and welcomed me into the family. It was such a magical evening. We sat around the table having drinks and desserts for almost two hours. Our families blended so well together. I had seriously hit the jackpot with this one. I didn't know it until this night, but "forever" was exactly what I needed.

39

When we finally decided to leave the restaurant, all I wanted to do was to take Katharine home to celebrate with her in private. Both of our kids had one more night before they went back to school, and we had already agreed not to spend the night together while our children were home. Sara and Emily said they were taking Jack and Martin to one of their favorite clubs, so I told them my driver could drop them off before he took Katharine and I to our respective apartments.

"Mom, why doesn't Ian spend the night at our place? Then he can join us for brunch before I go back to school. Sarah and Emily could join us too, if they don't have plans. How does that sound?" Jack asked.

"That's sounds like a great idea," Katharine said.

The girls and Martin agreed to come by Katharine's apartment at 11:30 a.m. I couldn't believe Jack had suggested I stay at their place. It was very thoughtful of him; I know it had to be strange for him to think of his mom sleeping with another man. His acceptance meant the world to me. I was so excited to celebrate our engagement properly.

We dropped the gang at the nightclub, which looked and sounded like it was packed. We could hear the pulsating music from our car. The kids jumped out of the car and instantly forgot about us. It was obvious they were ready to go party and dance. I know Jack and Sara weren't twenty-one yet, but I was pretty sure they both had believable fake IDs. I had never agreed with the legal drinking age, so it didn't bother me that they were going into the club. I was just thrilled that everyone got along so well. If I were honest about what I was seeing, I would speculate that there was something going on between Sara and Jack. I'd have to ask Katharine about that. I think she knew something I didn't.

My driver dropped Katharine and I off at her place, and I felt like a kid going to Disney. I started my sexual assault on her in the elevator. I couldn't help it. I had been waiting all night to get my hands on her. I pushed her against the wall and started thrusting my tongue into her mouth. She responded eagerly, which fueled my desire even more. I got my hands tangled in her hair so I could deepen the kiss. I had my body pressed against hers, but it didn't feel close enough. My right arm slid down her back and found her ass. I kneaded it and pulled her hips closer to mine. There was no way to hide how aroused I was. My hard body was poking against her midsection. She was moaning huskily. I felt like I was going to lose my mind.

A bell interrupted our intense make-out session, alerting us that we had reached our floor. Part of me wanted to stay in the elevator and make out with this sexy vixen for hours, but a bigger part of me wanted to get her naked and fuck her senseless.

We straightened up quickly, in case there was anyone on the other side of the door. Fortunately, there wasn't. We chased each other to her door, and she fumbled with her keys as she tried to unlock it. As she closed the door behind us, I pushed her against it and started kissing her passionately once again. I unbuttoned her shirt as she pushed off my suit coat and took off my tie. We undressed each other in record time, making sure our mouths never broke the seal. We sucked each other's mouths and necks as we panted in sexual frustration. I had never wanted this woman more than I wanted her at this very minute. Her acceptance of my proposal had been the strongest aphrodisiac of my life.

My heart was beating fast, and my obvious arousal was throbbing hard against Katharine's stomach. She reached down and stroked me, and I knew I couldn't wait any longer. I reached down quickly to make sure she was wet enough that I could enter her without any discomfort. She was swollen and dripping—it was so hot knowing she wanted me as much as I wanted her.

I lifted her hips up, and she wrapped her legs around my waist. I still had her back pressed up against the front door. Without any warning, I shoved myself inside of her as deep as I could. She let out a cry and a breathy "harder!" so I didn't let up. I think it was one of the most intense and frenzied moments in our relationship. It didn't take long for either of us to find our release. I buried my head in her neck and moaned as she threw her head back and made similar sounds. The orgasm had been incredibly intense for me, and it was obvious she was just as satisfied. As our breathing slowed down, I made sure our bodies stayed joined and carried her into the bedroom.

I laid her down gently on the bed and settled my body on top of hers. We started kissing again. She told me she loved me. I told her I loved her forever. We giggled and started making out all over again. I feasted on her neck, her lips and her breasts. She massaged my ass and rotated her hips beneath me. I could feel myself getting aroused again. I'd never recovered this quickly before, not even when I was a teenage boy. This woman did incredible things to me. I felt like I had won the lottery.

This round of lovemaking was slow and sexy as hell. I kept my body inside of her for nearly a half an hour as we danced to the rhythm of our heartbeats and breath. This woman was going to be my wife. A dream that I didn't even know I had was coming true. It was one of the happiest days of my life.

40

Never in a million years had I thought that Ian would propose to me so soon. We had only been together for a couple months, and the logical part of my brain was teeming with reservations about getting married again. It was all happening so fast. I had never been a spontaneous woman, and here I was, being more spontaneous than I had ever been in my life. It was incredible how my life had changed in such a short time. It was a bit overwhelming, but I couldn't have been any happier. Ian was my knight in shining armor and my savior. He saved me from my sad and lonely existence. Any logical reservations that I had were completely trumped by something more powerful than logic. My heart, on the other hand, wanted to spend the rest of my life with him. I knew that for a fact. I loved him. I couldn't imagine spending one night away from him. That's why I said yes. It was surreal. I had fallen in love again. I couldn't believe it.

I loved that Ian had wanted our children to be a part of the proposal. If I'd said no, he would have been incredibly embarrassed. I would never have turned him down, though. I loved him too much. It was such a bonus to have our children on board with our relationship. They seemed to really like each other and accepted the fact that Ian and I wanted to be together. I couldn't remember ever feeling so blessed.

After our second round of sex, I ran to the foyer and collected our clothing. I didn't need Jack to see our things thrown all over the entranceway when he got home from the club. Then I went into the kitchen and grabbed a bottle of champagne and two crystal flutes so we could continue our celebration. It was late, and I should have been tired, but I was so high on happiness that I wanted to savor every minute of it. I was giddy at the prospect of being engaged at this point in my life. It made me so happy. I wasn't ready for the celebration to end quite yet.

Ian was excited to see me walk into the room with champagne. He'd expected me to be tired, but I told him sleep was the last thing on my mind. He put some music on, and we drank champagne and giggled like school children. "Thank you for saying yes Katharine," he said to me. "How could I say no?" I replied. "You brought the best ammunition ever to the proposal, Ian. You brought our children. As long as they're all on board, then I would never have said no to you. I love you too much to have turned you down. I can't wait to be married to you." Before the bottle was finished, we were making out like horny teenagers.

We made love for another hour before we both collapsed in a euphoric heap. His stamina was unbelievable. I never had sore muscles from sex before, and I didn't think it was possible to climax as much as I had in the past few months. His extreme level of fitness made him a machine, and I was reaping the benefits of it. Tonight was no exception. It was the best possible way to celebrate our engagement. I woke up around nine to the smell of coffee and my man kissing my neck. He knew that was the best way to wake me up: getting my neck kissed turned me on more than just about anything, and I loved having a cup of coffee when I first got up. Damn, I could get used to this.

After I finished my coffee, we fooled around again. It was playful and fun. It seemed like every time we had sex, it was different. I loved that about our relationship. We showered and got dressed after we finished; we had plans to have brunch with the kids before they went back to school.

Brunch was fun. We had bright, outgoing children who loved to talk, debate, and challenge one another. It was the best way to start the union of our two families. Brunch lasted about two hours, and then we all went our separate ways with hugs and smiles all around. We promised to get together again for Christmas, and I thought about how happy I was to be looking forward to a holiday instead of dreading it. "I did it, Bryce," I thought. "Not only did I find passion again, I found another family to love."

The next couple of weeks were a combination of work, sex, and dinners all over town. On the weekends, we would often leave the city and drive to resorts, ski lodges, bed and breakfasts, or casinos. We were lucky we could afford to go wherever we wanted without worrying about the cost. Deciding who paid for things, however, became a constant bone of contention between us. One day we got in a heated discussion about who was going to pay for the weekend we had planned at the Foxwoods Casino in Connecticut.

"I'm the man, Katharine. You need to let me pay for these trips," Ian said.

"I don't want your money, Ian. I can afford to do things, too. We need to find a way to share the expenses. I don't ever want you to think I'm using you for your money. I'm not your ex, you know,"

"Don't ever compare yourself to that bitch. It pisses me off that you would even mention her name in the same sentence with yours. I know you don't want my money. Just call me old-fashioned—I want to be able to spoil you. It makes me feel funny having you pay for things."

"Well, it makes *me* feel funny to have you pay for everything. We need to figure out a way to be partners in every aspect of our relationship. It won't work if you insist on paying for everything. I'm a grown woman, and I can take care of myself. I'm not going to start relying on a man at this point in my life," I said to him insistently.

"Why is relying on me a sign of weakness? Why can't you just loosen up and enjoy the fact that I want to indulge your every whim?" he asked me.

"Because it makes me feel like a whore!" I told him.

"Are you kidding me? You're a successful, brilliant attorney who is more than capable of being self-sufficient. How the hell could you ever compare yourself to a whore?" he said in a loud, frustrated voice.

"It's just like the discussion about who's going to pay for our new apartment. I can't expect *you* to pay for the place where *we* are going to live together. It's just not right!" I yelled at him.

"Consider it a wedding present," he offered as a suggestion.

"A watch or a necklace is a wedding present, not a penthouse apartment in Manhattan!" I said in exasperation.

"You're being unreasonable, Katharine."

"And you're being chauvinistic!" I said angrily.

I stormed out of the living room, went into my bathroom, and started a bath. It was the first real fight we'd ever had. I didn't like it, but I felt very strongly that we should share our expenses. I knew he was incredibly wealthy. I also knew what his ex-wife had done to him. I didn't ever want there to be a resemblance between us. I didn't give a rat's ass what his net worth was. I loved him and not his wallet. God, he was infuriating.

As I calmed down in my lavender-scented bath salts, I decided that we needed to put some kind of closure on our disagreement or we'd never get any rest. We were intelligent and reasonable adults who just couldn't come to an agreement about the financial crap. And that was what it was—crap. We were both independently wealthy, and we were still fighting about money. I knew that I had to give in a little bit. He was old-fashioned in a lot of ways, and I'd always thought that his old-school views were very sweet. It was one of the things that had first drawn me to him. Now that I thought about it, it was still an endearing factor that made me love him even more. Then what the fuck were we fighting for? For a true gentleman—which he was—it was emasculating to let a woman have too much financial control. God, I felt so conflicted. On one hand, I enjoyed all of his pampering when we were dating. After my agonizing year alone after Bryce died, I cherished everything he did for me. But I knew that it would be unsettling to be "taken care of" when we were married. It just wasn't me. I needed us to be equals in every aspect of our relationship. I was proud of my success and needed to maintain a sense of independence or this would never work. Hiding in the bathroom wasn't the answer. I needed to make him understand how I felt. I dried off quickly, threw on my Yale T-shirt, and went out to find Ian and make this right.

What I found instead was very shocking; it scared me. He had left the apartment. I couldn't believe it. How could he walk out? That was the last thing I'd expected him to do. He had never walked out before. Then again, we'd never fought like this before. I felt like I had been punched in the stomach. That's when I saw the note on my pillow:

My Dearest Katharine,

I'm sorry we argued. It's hard for me not to want to take care of you in every aspect of our relationship. It was how I was raised and, frankly, it makes me feel good. But I understand your point of view and your need to be independent. I find your strength in your convictions admirable and, in fact, quite sexy. When you locked yourself in the bathroom, however, I figured it was your way of telling me that you needed a night alone. I didn't want to intrude on your space if you needed some privacy. Walking out of here is going to be very difficult, but maybe it'll help us calm down and gain some perspective. We will figure the money thing out, I promise you.

Please remember, you are my forever.

Love, Ian

It was the first night since our engagement that we didn't sleep together. The note sent me into a fit of tears. He was the sweetest man in the whole world, and I had pushed him away. Then again, I didn't think I was being unreasonable—was I? I didn't know. I was logical. I couldn't help it. Logistically, it didn't make any sense for him to shell out such a large sum of money for a place we would be living in together. It just felt wrong to me. I didn't want to feel indebted to him. I owned my apartment outright and could easily buy the new place as well. It didn't feel right to have him buy it. No matter how wealthy he was, it was still a lot of money.

I worked in a profession that was dominated by men. I took a lot of pride in becoming a partner in our firm and proving myself to be a kick-ass attorney that was respected and admired. I believed women could be as smart and as powerful as men. I could never be happy if I weren't in a relationship based on equality. This overwhelming need to be self-sufficient never occurred to me until Ian offered to buy us the multi-million dollar penthouse. Ever since I met Ian, I found myself learning new things about myself that I had never been cognizant of before. For the first time in my life, I was truly understanding who I was and what I wanted out of life. And I wanted Ian-more than anything.

I slept like shit that night—if you can even call the hours I laid there crying "sleep." I found myself reaching over to Ian's side of the bed constantly. I hated the fact that it was cold and empty. We were reasonable adults. There had to be a compromise. Was Ian being gentlemanly or stubborn? I quickly put the thought out of my head: Ian wasn't a stubborn man. He was thoughtful and considerate. I was the unreasonable one, the one who had stormed out of the room like an petulant child.

I gave up on sleep and got out of bed around four. I made a pot of coffee and took it into my bathroom so I could start getting ready for work. My job had always been my solace when things were hectic in my personal life. Bryce and I didn't have many obstacles to overcome, and I know I was very fortunate. But I think things are different when you are older. I'm more confident. I'm more determined. And I think I'm a little set in my ways, which has made me suck at compromising.

I left the apartment at 5:30 a.m. and stopped at my favorite deli for a bagel, lox, and cream cheese sandwich. I knew that I would need some food to keep my energy up. I checked my phone constantly, hoping for a text from Ian, but was disappointed every time. He probably didn't want to wake me up. Little did he know that he needn't have worried—a person needs to sleep in order to be woken up.

I was sitting at my desk by 6:30 a.m., deciding what to do. Ian had left me a note, so I knew the next move was up to me. After fiddling with the numbers on my phone for what seemed like forever, I called him.

"Morning, counselor," he said in the quiet, dreamy voice that could make me swoon even when things weren't perfect between us.

"Hey there. I'm so sorry about last night. You mad at me?" I asked nervously.

"Of course not. I love you, Katharine. You are my forever. I mean that. I guess we had to expect a few bumps along the way. We'll figure this out. I came up with a few ideas last night that I'd like to discuss with you. Are you free for dinner?" he asked eagerly.

"You bet. I feel like such a bitch. I shouldn't have locked you out. It was childish and wrong. You're my forever, too. Please say you forgive me. I missed you last night," I admitted shyly.

"Last night sucked. I don't ever want to spend another night without you. I can't take it. From this day forward, I vow to resolve my issues with you or sleep on the couch," he said with a laugh.

"Well, if you sleep on the couch, you'd better make room for me, because I'll be sleeping there with you," I told him.

"I can live with that. How's seven for dinner?"

"That works. Meet you at Todd's?"

"It's a date."

And with that, we ended the call.

41

I was so glad Katharine called me. I'd been up all night waiting to hear from her. I was also happy that she'd agreed to meet me tonight. I'd been scared she would need more time to cool off. Last night had been horrible. It was our first disagreement, and I prayed it was our last. I didn't ever want to spend another night without her. I loved her so much and hated any time apart from her.

I'd been thinking all night about the best way to resolve this issue. I had the money. Shit, I had more money than I could ever spend. It was stupid that it had even become an issue. But Katharine was a proud and independent woman. I loved that about her. The last thing I wanted to do was make her feel uncomfortable about our living situation. I knew she wasn't after my money, and I understood why she wouldn't let me just buy the new place and be done with it. I didn't know exactly how financially secure she was, and I didn't care. I wanted to be a good provider. It was how my father raised me. Besides, it was silly to fight over the logistics when I could easily afford to buy it. But I did understand where she was coming from, and I had to admit, her need to be equals in this relationship was sexy as hell. After hours of scrutinizing our problem, I came up with a plan that I hoped she would agree to.

She was waiting at the bar when I arrived at the restaurant. I knew I'd never get over admiring what a beautiful woman she was. She was dressed in a beautiful designer suit that was tailored perfectly to her body. Her hair was in a twist, showing off her sexy neck—I wanted to bite it. As usual, she had high heels on to keep her look more feminine. To me, they were an invitation to hot, steamy sex. In fact, if all went well tonight, I wanted to make love to her in nothing but those heels.

"You have a naughty look on your face, Ian," Katharine said quietly to me as I approached her.

I leaned toward her and gave her a chaste kiss. I didn't want to be presumptuous and come on too strong. I had to laugh at her remark. I wasn't exactly sure how I should respond, since my mind was indeed filled with very naughty, very erotic thoughts.

"I think I'll plead the fifth," I said judiciously.

"Oh no you don't—'fess up. What's going on in that brain of yours, Mr. Jensen?"

I didn't want to say anything out loud, so I leaned in and whispered in her ear. I was very specific about the image that was in my mind. First, I told her she looked beautiful, because that was my initial thought as I walked into the restaurant and saw her sitting at the bar. Second, I told her that I wanted to suck on her neck and leave marks on it like a lovesick teenager, because the way her hair was twisted up looked like an invitation for me to devour. I told her that I had never seen an attorney look so incredibly hot in my entire life. She made a classic suit look like a strip tease outfit. I continued by telling her that she would look even more beautiful getting slammed by me while wearing nothing but her sexy heels. She burst out laughing and turned her body toward me so she could hug me properly. Being honest with Katharine turned out to be the best icebreaker ever.

We decided to stay at the bar and order some food. The bartenders were fun, and it wasn't that busy at the end of the bar where we were sitting. I ordered a drink for myself since she already had one, and we decided on a few appetizers. I decided to get the business part of the

evening over with so we could just enjoy each other and talk about sub-
jects that didn't cause tension between us.

"I have an idea. Why don't we form a legal partnership and buy the
apartment together as a formal, business entity? We'll both pay half. If
that's too much, then you could always get a loan for the balance. I have a
feeling your current place will sell for close to that amount, if not more,
so you wouldn't have to owe very much. I would hate for you to cash in
on any of your investments to purchase the apartment. I don't know what
kind of cash flow you have access to, and it's really none of my business.
What you bring to this marriage will remain yours and Jack's, regardless of how long you and I remain together. My prayer is that we'll be
together forever, but I'm trying to protect us both and to be realistic as
well. I don't ever want money to cause animosity between us. All I want
from you is your love. The way the partnership will work is that if one
of us passes, our children will inherit our half. This way, money should
never come between us again. How does my idea sound?"

I thought about his proposal for a minute before I answered. "Well,
it sounds like you thought this through very carefully, and that makes
me very happy. Yesterday, I felt like you were trying to bully me into ac-
cepting your generosity, and it made me feel very uncomfortable. I like
being financially independent; it is a part of who I am. I could never
be beholden to you financially. It just feels wrong to me. Please don't
misunderstand me though. Offering to buy the apartment was very generous, and I understand and appreciate your inherent need to be the
provider. It is endearing, to say the least. It actually makes me love you
even more, even if I can't accept it. Anyway, as it turns out, Bryce had a
very large life insurance policy when he died. We also owned my place
free and clear. I make a very lucrative wage at the firm and have made
more money than I could probably ever spend. I think your suggestion
of forming a partnership is brilliant, and I accept your offer to develop a
business entity together. By the way, I'm flattered by how much you want
to protect Jack and me. Your concern for my welfare is actually kind of
hot, and if we weren't in public, I would show you how appreciative I am."

"I plan to hold you to that later tonight, counselor. First, we need to come up with a name for our corporation so I can file the papers tomorrow. Any thoughts?" I asked her.

"How about G&T, Inc.?" she suggested. It was a name that instantly came to me.

I laughed. "It's perfect. Hell, if it wasn't for that gin and tonic, we never would have found each other. G&T it is," I said happily.

42

Ian was a brilliant businessman, and I knew he would come up with a solution that would be acceptable to me. I loved the idea of being partners, both in business and in love. We vowed that last night was going to be the last night we would spend apart. I loved him too much to go another day without him.

Now I had to deal with my next dilemma. I needed to tell Bryce's parents that I was getting married again. I spoke to them occasionally, and our conversations always led back to memories of their son. Then the reminiscing would cause his mom to cry. They weren't dealing well with the loss, and I couldn't blame them. I don't think I could ever get over losing my son. It had been hard for me to have conversations with them since Bryce died, but I was determined to keep them updated on their grandson. Jack made a point of stopping by their house every once in a while, and I called with updates on college whenever something important happened.

Since Ian was such a powerful figure in New York City, and my partnership in the law firm had also made me fairly well known, there was no way our wedding wouldn't make some kind of news. I would have hated for them to find out about our wedding from the television or newspaper; it would have broken their hearts. I thought the best way to approach them was in person.

I called them early in the week and asked if I could stop by on Saturday around lunchtime. It had been a long time since we had actually seen each other in person, and they seemed very excited to see me. When I pulled into the driveway, I noticed the engagement ring on my hand. There was no way they could miss it—it was stunning. I decided to put it in my purse.

Bryce's parents greeted me with hugs and what seemed liked forced smiles. I could feel their exhaustion and despair. They looked much older and sadder than I remembered, and it was heartbreaking. We went into the kitchen, and Mrs. Collins poured us all a cup of coffee. After ten minutes of small talk, Mrs. Collins asked me why I had stopped by. I had been a part of their lives for thirty years, and she knew me almost as well as my own mom did. I took a deep breath and prayed for the courage to tell them.

"I have something to tell you, and I wanted to do it in person. I'm going to—I've met someone, and we plan to get married next summer," I said quietly.

"How could you? Our baby isn't even cold in the grave, and you're just moving on without a care in the world!" Mrs. Collins shouted at me. She stood up so abruptly that the chair she was sitting on fell over behind her. The noise was startling. This was not what I'd expected.

"This past year and a half has been excruciating for me. I wasn't eating or sleeping. I felt like I was dying, too. I loved Bryce with all my heart for thirty years. This hasn't been an easy decision for me." I was pleading with them, trying not to burst into tears. It wasn't working.

"That's crap, and you know it! If you loved my son, you would honor his memory and not move on like a two-bit hussy!" she screamed at me.

"Sandra, please," Bryce's father interjected, "calm down. You're not being fair. You know Katie loved our Bryce. Her being alone isn't going to bring him back. Remember the last time Katie and Jack came to visit? You commented on how thin and sad Katie looked. You even wondered whether or not you should ask her if she was having health problems. It's good to see her looking like her old self again. She needs to be there for our grandson. I know this is hard, but she has the right to be happy."

"What about our rights? I don't think I'll ever be happy again. And what do I have to be fair about? Our boy is dead. Dead! Now I have to wonder if you ever truly loved my son at all. And how does Jack feel? I imagine he is as devastated as we are. How can you do this to him? I never expected you to be so selfish." She started to sob.

A long, painful moment passed before I tried to speak. "I'm sorry you feel that way. I loved your son more than anything in the world, and I'll never forget him. I see him every time I look in Jackson's eyes. I'm sorry to have upset you; that was not my intent. I just thought you should know what I was doing. I love you both and hope you don't take your anger out on Jack. You are his grandparents, and he loves you very much."

Without waiting for their response, I stood up and left the house. I started the car and drove to the end of the block. When I got to the first stop sign, I put the car in park, turned off the engine, and started sobbing hysterically. I had known they wouldn't be thrilled with my news, but I hadn't expected to be attacked like I was. How could they think I didn't love their son? I loved him with every fiber of my being. It wasn't fair for them to expect me to mourn the rest of my life. I didn't regret my decision, but I hadn't expected to feel guilty about it. God, this really sucked. Didn't they realize that I was barely functioning before Ian came into my life? I was lucky I hadn't died of malnourishment and a severely broken heart. I would always love their son, but I'd made him a promise. And it was a promise I intended to keep.

43

I got the most frantic phone call from Katharine. She was driving home from the Collinses', and it didn't sound like it had gone well. I could barely make out what she was saying, so I just told her that I would meet her at my place. I was afraid that her apartment might hold too many memories at the moment; she sounded very fragile. I had never heard her so distraught. Her sobs were so intense that it sounded like she was hiccupping between every breath. She kept trying to reiterate the things Bryce's mom had said to her, but her speech was barely audible. I tried to talk to her calmly, so she wouldn't get into an accident. It scared me that she had to make the drive back from Connecticut by herself. I talked to her for several minutes, until her sobbing subsided.

I was able to get home before she got there. I filled a tub, opened a bottle of wine, and put soft music on. When she walked though my front door, she dropped her purse on the floor and ran into my arms. She sobbed into my chest, and I just held her. When she started to calm down, I walked her to the kitchen to fetch a glass of wine. She told me about all of the awful things Mrs. Collins had said to her. It was obvious that her in-laws weren't dealing well with their son's passing. I told her I was proud of her for going there to tell them her plans for the future. I continued to rub her back as we talked, and eventually I felt her calming down.

In order to bring some levity into the room, I asked her, "She really called you a 'two-bit hussy'?"

"Yes. It was awful," she said quietly. "Why couldn't they have been a little understanding? My parents loved Bryce too, but they were able to be happy for us when we told them we were engaged. They saw how heartbroken I was after he died. That was why they thanked you. They were able to understand that you brought me another chance to find some happiness in my life. God, it was so horrible, Ian."

I wrapped my arms around her. "You can be my two-bit hussy every day of the week, wench. Your—*hussery* is one of your more endearing qualities," I teased her.

"Why thank you, Mr. Jensen. I've never seen myself in that particular light, but I'll try to live up to the highest standards of hussiness, if it makes you happy." She gave me a small smile.

"How about a hot bubble bath?" I asked her.

"That would be nice. Would you please join me? I don't want to be alone."

"That was the plan all along," I replied.

Katharine was able to talk more calmly once we were in the tub drinking our second glass of wine. When I asked her if she was reconsidering her decision, she emphatically said that she couldn't wait to marry me. She felt terrible that she had brought her in-laws more pain, but that didn't sway her decision one way or the other. She loved me, and nothing would change that fact. That made me feel so much better. Intellectually, she knew that Bryce was never coming back to her. On the other hand, she still loved him and missed him very much. I understood her conflict. I didn't feel threatened that Katharine still loved her husband; I just felt blessed to have met her, and I knew she felt the same way. We were both very lucky to have found one another.

We spent too much time in the tub, and the water began to cool off. I suggested we light a fire and order some takeout. She agreed to both. I knew she wouldn't want to go out, and I didn't have enough food in the fridge to make a decent meal. There was a gourmet restaurant a few blocks away that delivered; we'd found it when we first started having sleepovers, and it had become our favorite. Tonight, she ordered a Caesar salad with grilled shrimp, and I ordered chicken French. I knew she wouldn't want anything heavy, because her stomach was still upset from her meeting with her in-laws.

Dinner was great, and we snuggled on the couch drinking wine once we finished our meals. We talked for hours, until I could feel Katharine's body getting heavy. She was completely drained. I picked her up and carried her to the bedroom, then I helped her undress and tucked her under the covers. I sat next to her on the bed and gave her a loving kiss.

"Aren't you going to join me?" she asked sadly.

"Right now, you need to sleep. Today was a tough day for you, and I can feel your exhaustion. I want you wide awake when I make love to that scrumptious body of yours."

"Could you lie with me until I fall asleep?" she asked quietly.

"Of course."

I crawled in next to her, and she rested her head on my chest. I stroked her hair and reminded her how much I loved her and how brave I thought she was. Within minutes, she was sound asleep. I snuck out to clean up the dishes and turn off the fireplace. I brushed my teeth for a long time, daydreaming about her. When I snapped out of my reverie, I decided to shave my face so I'd be nice and smooth for her in the morning.

I was already thinking about how I would wake her, with my mouth between her beautiful legs. She preferred my face cleanly shaven when I went down on her, so I shaved more often when I planned to do that. Hell, it was the least I could do.

44

I fell asleep feeling bad about upsetting Bryce's parents, but I could never have predicted their reaction. I was still glad I'd told them in person, even if it did make them angry. I needed them to know I would always love their son, but I was tired of being sad. I felt so blessed to have found love again. And I did love Ian so very much.

I opened my eyes, feeling calmer. That sense of dread had left my heart. I had done the right thing, and I didn't want to feel bad or guilty anymore. I rolled over on my side and watched Ian sleep. He was such a beautiful man. I was so incredibly lucky. It was time to repay him for being so sweet last night.

Ian knew that kissing my neck was the best way to wake me up. I had a feeling he would respond even more favorably if I kissed something else on his body in order to wake him up. I snuck my head under the covers and found what I was looking for. I started sucking him gently and lovingly; I didn't want to startle him. As he grew bigger, I felt his hand tangling in my hair as he started rubbing my head. Yeah, he was up. I increased my suction and buried myself between his legs. I massaged his balls and played with that special area between his sac and his ass. I felt him squirming and getting more aroused. His veins started throbbing, and I had to decide whether I was going to finish him off this way or climb on top of him.

"That was how I had planned to wake _you_ up, Katharine," he said to me sleepily. "It appears you beat me to it."

"This hussy couldn't wait for her master's lazy ass to wake up, so I figured I'd better take things into my own hands," I chuckled.

I continued my oral assault on him for several more minutes before my own selfishness took over. I wanted to experience pleasure with him. Sucking on him made me wanton and wet, and I couldn't wait to climb on top of him. I climbed up his body slowly, kissing as much of him as possible. I was happy he was naked, so I didn't have to waste any time taking any of his clothes off.

When I got to his face, he started kissing me deeply. His kisses alone could bring me to orgasm. He knew just the right pressure to bring goose bumps to my skin and a throbbing between my legs. As our kissing became more intense, I lowered myself on top of him. It was a perfect fit.

I started slowly, wanting to enjoy every sensation my body was feeling. That didn't last very long. We had such amazing chemistry that the tempo quickly escalated. He grabbed my hips in order to push my body deeper onto his. I was close to the brink, but I wanted us to climax at the same time.

"Ian, I'm so close..." I said in a ragged breath.

"Let go. I plan to join you...now!"

That was all it took. We found our release at the same time. It was electrifying. As our breathing started to slow down, I curled up next to him, and we just held each other. I loved making love to this hunk of a man. I knew I'd never regret my decision to marry him. He'd brought me back to life.

45

hristmas was approaching, and I wanted to do something really special for Katharine; she had been working long hours at the firm. We still hadn't made any concrete plans for the wedding. We knew we wanted to do it when our kids were home from school, which is why we were talking about next summer. Although she was eating better and working out, she looked tired. I needed to figure out an escape so she could rest and be rejuvenated. I had confirmed with all three children that we were going to spend Christmas together. Emily had two weeks off from school, and the other two had nearly a month off. Then I got an idea.

I called the kids and asked their opinions. Everyone was on board. Since our first weekend at Bear Mountain, I knew that Katharine didn't mind being spontaneous and she seemed to love surprises. Over the past months, I had planned several new things for us to do together at the last minute. We had fun on every adventure I was able to come up with thus far. She was asking for turns to plan things as well. Every weekend was something different. We were having so much fun together. Now that I was sure Katharine loved surprises, I was pretty confident that this was going to be the ultimate surprise.

I told Katharine that the plan was for all of us to spend the night at my apartment on Christmas Eve so we could be together Christmas morning. Katharine thought the kids were coming at noon for brunch, but everybody was going to be arriving ridiculously early. I also told her that I had arranged for food to be brought in so she wouldn't have to cook anything. In reality, they were all going to meet at my place at eight that morning. I had packed a travel bag full of her things and hidden it in my closet. At eight o'clock sharp, there was a knock at the door. Katharine and I were in our pajamas having coffee and hanging out in the kitchen when they arrived. She was thrilled to see everyone but suspicious as to why they were so early. I told her that since my girls had become adults, we preferred opening gifts on Christmas Eve and going to church on Christmas morning. That wasn't exactly true, but it was all part of our plan. I made more coffee, and we went to the living room to exchange gifts. Katharine seemed to forget that everyone had arrived early. There was a lot of laughter, and I couldn't have been happier about the camaraderie among our children.

The last gift to be opened was one that I had bought for Katharine. It was a small box, and she stared at it quizzically for a few minutes. The kids were snickering, and Katharine looked around at all of us with renewed suspicion. I prompted her to open it; we had to get going. She unwrapped the package slowly, almost as if she was nervous about what might be inside. When she opened the box, her eyes filled with tears. I had gotten us wedding bands. Hers was an eternity ring, set all around with a row of diamonds weighing a total of four karats. I loved the notion of an eternity ring; it seemed the most fitting to me. Mine was platinum with a row of diamonds in the center. She looked at me, confused.

"It's time to make you my forever," I told her.

All the kids were smiling, and Katharine started to cry. She stood up and hugged me, then went around and hugged each of the kids. When the hugs were over, she walked over to me and took my hands in hers.

"I can't wait to be your forever," she said quietly.

"That's good, because it's about to happen. Take a quick shower and get dressed. We are going on an adventure," I told her.

"Where are we going?" she asked, looking around at the group.

"It's a surprise. Now hurry up and get ready. We have to leave by ten at the latest, or we'll miss our ride," I pushed her along to the bedroom.

The kids were still laughing as they cleaned up the wrapping paper and coffee cups. I was so happy that they all supported our union. They had kept their bags downstairs with the valet so Katharine wouldn't see them. While she was in the shower, I had both of our suitcases taken downstairs. Jack made sure all the bags were put into the limousine that was waiting to take us to the airport and came back up to let me know everything was ready. I picked out an outfit for Katharine to wear, which surprised her, but she went along with it.

Once we were all piled into the limo, Katharine badgered the kids for information, but no one was budging. I opened a bottle of champagne, so we toasted our adventure, even though Katharine was still in the dark. I was so happy I'd been able to find her passport. I'd brought up the subject one day, wanting to make sure she had one for our honeymoon—or so I told her. Thankfully, it was right where she said it was.

There was hardly any traffic, and we got to the airport in record time. Katharine seemed very surprised when she saw the small plane waiting for us.

"Where are we going?" she asked.

"It's a surprise, Mom," said Jack. "I promise you'll love it."

We boarded the most beautiful private jet I had ever been on. There were two private rooms with beds, as well as two bathrooms equipped with showers—this was the way to travel. I could tell Katharine had a million questions, but she stayed quiet and just kept smiling. I would have to plan more adventures like this if they would get her to smile like she was now. A flight attendant offered us mimosas or Bloody Marys, and everyone chose something to drink. I had a feeling we'd all be sleeping most of the ride if we kept drinking. The kids were excited and were chatting incessantly about the most random things. I was so glad they were as excited about this trip as I was.

Katharine tugged at my shirt and asked if we were flying overseas. I told her we were, and that I had brought her passport. She teased me about being sneaky and going behind her back, but I could tell she was as excited as I was. The crew gave us our safety instructions as we reached cruising altitude, and brunch was served. We had clams casino for an appetizer. I had several bottles of an Italian wine brought on board to accompany our meal. I didn't know if she would get the hint, but our kids certainly did—they burst out laughing when the crew poured us each a glass. Katharine didn't know why they were laughing, but she enjoyed their festive mood. Our next course was a mixed green salad. For the main course, they served us filet mignon, roasted potatoes, and asparagus with hollandaise sauce. The food was excellent, as was the wine and the company. It took us over an hour to eat, and by the time we were done, everyone was getting sleepy. My girls retired to one room, Katharine and I went into the other, and Jack slept on a reclining lounge chair.

We had about seven more hours of flying time, so a nap was just what we all needed.

46

I had no idea what Ian had planned, and frankly, I couldn't have cared less. I was with the people I loved the most in the world. I had only known the girls for a few months, but I felt like they were truly a part of my family. I spoke to them all of the time. Sara and I went to lunch whenever possible, and Emily was constantly texting me about her internship, law school, and even her relationship with Martin. It was obvious that they had lousy relationships with their mom, and I was happy I could be there for them. There were just some things a girl didn't want to talk to her dad about. I was so glad when they started reaching out to me. It made me feel like they really wanted me to be a part of their family.

Brunch was spectacular, but drinking that early in the day took its toll on everybody. Even though I had no idea where we were going, I knew it would take several hours to get there. Ian and I said our goodnights and retired to one of the bedrooms. We lay on the bed and started kissing.

"This was the most thoughtful gift, Ian. It's very extravagant but amazing nonetheless. Thank you for arranging all of this," I said to him.

"You don't even know where we're going," he replied.

"It doesn't matter. All I care about is that the five of us are together. I'd be happy flying around in circles over whatever ocean is below us and calling it a day. I just love being with all of you. That's the best gift you could ever give me," I said honestly.

"Well, I guess I could cancel the rest of the trip, but I think our children would be very disappointed. Besides, I think you're going to like what I have planned. This is only the start of our adventure—and our life together."

"If you don't mind, I'll withhold judgment for now. Instead, how about we join the mile high club?" I asked playfully.

"I thought you'd never ask."

47

After several hours, everyone started to wake up, and another meal was served. We sat around the table, talking and laughing. It was obvious that our children were excited about the week ahead of them. Katharine tried fishing for hints, but none of them were budging. This was turning out to be even more fun than I imagined.

The pilot said that we were beginning our descent into Rome, and Katharine looked at me with wide eyes. "We're going to Italy?" she asked.

"Yes ma'am," I replied. "I hope the country is to your liking?"

"To my liking?" she scoffed. "It's my favorite country in the whole world!" She wrapped her arms around me and gave me the biggest hug imaginable.

There was a limousine waiting for us when we finished going through customs. The process was very efficient, and we were on our way in no time at all. The limousine was stocked with chilled champagne and exquisite Italian snacks. We ate Caprese salad and Italian meats and cheeses. The energy in the limo was electrifying.

The ride through wine country never ceased to amaze me; Italy was so beautiful. I had rented a luxurious home in Tuscany with a full kitchen and household staff. It would be a week full of good food and wine, beautiful vistas, and every possible amenity imaginable. What was going to make the vacation even more perfect was the other surprise I had planned: I would be asking Katharine to accept my proposal once again and to marry me in one of the most beautiful churches in the Tuscan Valley.

We all got settled in and had a relaxing rest of the day lounging around. The long flight and overflowing glasses of wine had everyone asleep shortly after the sun set over the magnificent vineyards.

The master bedroom had a wall of glass windows and doors. The view was spectacular, and it was completely private. I made love to Katharine slowly and lovingly, and we fell asleep wrapped in each other's arms. When we woke up, the sun was starting to rise. We went to the enclosed greenhouse with its billowing couches and watched the sunrise. One of the staff brought us cappuccinos and pastries and then disappeared so we could have our privacy.

When we finished our coffee, I took the cup out of Katharine's hand. I took both of her hands in mine and turned my body so I was completely facing her. She had a look of concern on her face.

"Ian, what's the matter?" she asked sympathetically.

"I have to tell you something important, and I have to ask you something. I still can't believe I found you. What I need to tell you is that I love you more than any woman I have ever loved in my entire life. The day you said yes to my marriage proposal was one of the happiest days I can remember. Now, here, with all of our children gathered together, in the most beautiful place in the world, I'd like to make it official. Ms. Katharine Collins, would you do me the honor and the privilege of becoming my beloved wife? I would like to marry you today. Please say yes. It would make me the happiest man in the entire world."

"Oh Ian," she gasped through her tears, "I'd love to, but I don't have a dress."

"Actually, you do. The girls contacted the friend you get the designer clothes from, and rumor has it that there's a gown, shoes, and everything else you might need in the guest bedroom. Sara and Emily took care of all of the details. All you need to do is say yes."

Katharine switched positions and crawled onto my lap. She put her arms around my neck and kissed me.

"There is nothing I would rather do than become your wife. Today. In Italy. With our children. Oh God, Ian. I love you so much!"

Only moments later, we heard cheering and clapping. The gang had been hiding behind us and had heard Katharine agree to my proposal. They came running into the room. We stood up, the girls crying and hugging. They grabbed Katharine and dragged her to the guest room where her dress was waiting. Jack and I stood there and watched them leave. When I looked back at him, he had tears in his eyes.

"Thank you for making my mother so happy, Ian," he said to me.

"No, I want to thank you. Your mother has made *me* so happy, and I can't thank you enough for letting me be a part of your lives. I love her so much, Jackson. I promise I will take good care of her and love her forever."

I walked over to my fiancé's son and gave him a hug. We started to laugh and walked out of the greenhouse to get some breakfast.

48

The girls were squealing as we ran up to the guest room. They couldn't wait to show me the dress that my girlfriend had shipped to the villa. Sara and Emily had gone online and picked out a couple of dresses they thought I would like from the selection Gabriella had sent them. She had been able to figure out which dress would work best with my body type, and she also knew what designers I liked the best. She had decided on a Lebanese fashion designer named Georges Chakra. His designs were stunning. I had originally seen him at Paris Fashion Week and had been a fan ever since. I hadn't worn many of his designs, but I had mentioned him to Gabriella once. Now I was glad I had: the dress was spectacular.

The girls had me try the dress on to make sure it fit—Ian had a seamstress on call in case any alterations needed to be made. It fit perfectly, and all three of us burst into tears once it was buttoned up. Then I asked what they were wearing. My girlfriend had sent the girls two awesome Vera Wang dresses. All they'd had to do was send their measurements to her, and she'd made sure the dresses were a perfect fit. Sara had picked out a soft blue dress, and Emily had decided on a pale yellow one. They told me that Gabriella had sent suits for the men, too. Apparently, the clothing was a wedding present to us. I needed to call her when I got the chance and thank her.

The ceremony was set for four o'clock, so they helped me change out of my dress, and we went back downstairs to join the guys for breakfast. We sat around the breakfast table for nearly two hours. Nothing was rushed in Italy, which was a welcome change from the constant hustle of New York City. The relaxed way of life was one of the many reasons I loved Italy so much.

We collectively decided that we needed some exercise, so we all went to change so we could go for a long walk through the quaint town. We were all anxious to check out the church we were going to get married in later in the day.

Everything was happening so fast, and I couldn't have been happier. As Ian and I were dressing for our hike, he came behind me and enveloped me into a huge hug.

"Happy?" he asked me.

"Deliriously," I told him.

"Want to show me?" he asked playfully.

"Not a chance. You have to wait for the wedding night," I scolded.

"I'm not sure I'll be able to wait that long," he whined.

"That's just too bad. I'm not letting you sample the goods until you've purchased the mule," I laughed.

"Mule? Woman, you've lost your senses." We were still laughing as we went downstairs to join our party.

49

We roamed around the town for over an hour before we got to the church where the ceremony was to be held. Italy was known for its thousands of churches, nestled in picturesque nooks throughout the country. I had come across this particular church when I was traveling in the area with my daughters three years ago. Built in the fifteenth century, it was a small church with ornate stained glass designs and marble statues. As soon as Katharine walked in, her eyes filled with tears. It was a cozy and intimate church full of history and charm. I knew she would love it. I found a bilingual priest willing to perform the ceremony, and he was going to have all of the legal documents waiting at the church for us to sign.

We stood gazing at the alter for a long time, just hugging. Jack was going from statue to statue admiring the craftsmanship. Whoever had designed this magnificent relic of a building was an incredibly talented architect and artist. Every square inch of the church had something beautiful to admire.

"How'd you find this place?" Jack asked me.

"I brought the girls here three years ago. We were roaming around the area, and we made it our mission to go into every church we could find. We couldn't get over how different every church we came across was. We just couldn't seem to get our fill. When we came across this particular one, we sat down in the pews for the longest time, just admiring its beauty. To say that the churches in the United States pale in comparison is a gross understatement. The people who built the churches in Italy were true artisans, especially since the structures were built hundreds of years ago, and it had to be so much more difficult to construct these magnificent works of art. We agreed that this church was our favorite. At one point, Sara made the comment that she would love to get married here one day. That thought made me smile. Never in a million years did I ever picture myself being the one to get married here, but here we are. I'm experiencing a dream that I didn't even know I had six months ago. It's surreal," I commented reflectively.

We all agreed that this was the perfect place to get married. Everyone was starting to get hungry, so we wandered back to the villa to have lunch before we started getting ready for the ceremony. The staff had prepared a fantastic spread for us. Food tasted so much better in Italy; everything was so fresh and delicious. Once we had our fill, I gave Katharine one last kiss, and we went our separate ways to get ready.

The girls had advised me that they would need about two hours to get ready. Jack and I decided that we wouldn't need that long, so we went to the veranda to hang out and relax for a while. I didn't get a lot of time with Jack at home, so I took advantage of this time we had together. It was obvious that he was a bright young man with a lot of ambition. It was also obvious that he loved his mother very much and had felt very protective of her since his father passed. I was looking forward to having a son in my life.

We didn't have any problem finding things to talk about. He was an easygoing young man, and I liked him a lot. At one point, however, the conversation stalled, and he was looking at me strangely.

"What's up?" I asked him. It was obvious he wanted to say something to me.

"I want to talk to you about something. But I need to preface it by saying that my mom and I have an honesty pact. We're honest with one another even if it threatens to upset the other person. It's important that I know you'll be honest with me, too," he said cautiously.

"OK. I promise to be honest with you, regardless of how I may think it may make you feel. Fair enough?" I asked him.

"Fair enough," Jack said. "This is the thing. Oh, this is hard..."

"Just spit it out, Jackson. You can ask me anything," I encouraged him, even though I was a little nervous about what he was going to say.

"OK, here it is. I'm crazy about Sara, and I'd like to ask her on a date, but only if I have your permission and your blessing."

Wow, I hadn't seen that one coming. I gave myself a minute to think about it before answering. How did I feel about our children dating? The notion had never crossed my mind. Sure, there had been moments when I was startled by their affection, but Sara was such a demonstrative girl, I hadn't really given it a second thought.

"I didn't see this coming, Jackson. To be honest, I'm not sure how I feel about it, if you want my initial reaction. You two don't have a biological connection, but we have merged our families. Then again, I haven't been crazy about her boyfriends in the past, and I already like you. It seems a little unorthodox, I guess, but it doesn't seem like it should be taboo or wrong. How does Sara feel?" I asked him.

"I'm not totally sure. We've gone out a few times without you guys, and we always have such a good time together. I have been really careful not to allow it to go any further, because I didn't want it to be weird. More importantly, I really didn't want to screw up what you and Mom have. I've told her all about it, but I asked her not to say anything to you because I wanted to speak to you directly. I was just waiting for a time when we could be alone, when no one would barge in on us."

"This is a surprise, but not an unwelcome one. I think I'm fine with it, Jackson. If my daughter is interested in dating you, you have my blessing. I'll warn you that she can be quite a handful. She is impetuous and has absolutely no control of what comes out of her mouth. The beauty is that she is also honest to a fault and life will never be boring. You and Sara? Interesting. Good luck, son. I hope it turns out the way you two want it."

We stood up, shook hands, and went our separate ways to get ready for the wedding. What an interesting twist to the day: Jackson and Sara.

50

Oh my God, was I glad that was over. I'd wanted to get Ian alone to talk to him pretty much since Thanksgiving, and I never could find the right moment. There was no way I was waiting any longer, though: Sara and I had gotten to the point where we talked almost every day, and I really wanted to take her on a proper date. If Ian hadn't wanted me to, though, I would have backed off. It was more important that my mom be happy.

Now I didn't have to wait any longer. I needed to decide the best way to approach Sara. It was obvious that she liked me, too, but I only hoped it didn't freak her out—after all, our folks were getting hitched in about an hour. One hour? Holy crap, I needed to get ready!

51

Ian arranged for separate cars to take us to the church; Emily had told me that he didn't want to see me in my dress before I walked down the aisle. Jackson checked in on me right before he was getting ready to leave. He asked the girls for a moment alone with me before everyone left. He needed to make sure I was ready and certain this was what I wanted to do. I told him that I couldn't wait to marry Ian. I think he just needed to be certain and to hear me say it one last time. He also was anxious to tell me that he had finally gotten the chance to talk to Ian in private.

"Ian gave me the thumbs-up on the Sara thing, Mom. I'm so happy right now," he beamed.

"I'm glad, sweetheart. I never said anything to him. Was he surprised?" I asked.

"Oh yeah. It took him a minute to process everything. I mean, it *is* kind of weird. But he gave me his permission. Now I just need to ask her out. We're in, like, the most romantic place on the planet, so maybe I'll do it before we leave—I don't know. Anyway, this is your day. I'm really happy for you. And you look like a queen in that gown. Who knew a guy from Beirut could come up with something so beautiful and elegant? The dress rocks, Mom, and so do you."

He kissed me on the cheek and disappeared. The girls came in to make sure everything was all right, and I assured them that everything was perfect. It was fun having them around. I really liked having daughters. We got the rest of our things together and headed out the door.

I heard an organ playing as we pulled up to the church. The music added so much to the historic splendor of this magical place. Ian said that the ceremony would be brief. The priest would say a blessing, we would say our own vows, and then we would receive communion. After one final blessing, we would be man and wife. It was happening so fast, but it felt incredibly right.

The vows were, by far, the best part of the ceremony. Ian spoke first. "My dearest Katharine, you have completed my life by filling my heart with laughter and love. Before I met you, I had accepted the fact that I would spend of the rest of my life alone. You gave me hope and made me believe in love again. You brought me a dream I didn't know I had. You brought joy to my somber existence and filled my life with sunshine. I had lost all faith in happy endings, but you restored my faith with your unselfish love and trust. I didn't realize how lonely I was until I met you. Thank you for agreeing to be my forever."

It took me a minute to compose myself before I was able to speak. "My dearest Ian, you brought me out of the depths of despair. If it hadn't been for my beautiful son, Jackson, I would have perished long before I had the chance to meet you. You turned the light on in my very dark and lonely world. I no longer believed in fairytale endings, but you made me believe in magic again. You have given me strength when I felt weak, solace when I felt uncertainty, and love—unconditionally. You also brought me two daughters I cherish with all my heart. Most importantly, you brought me forever. For that, I will be eternally grateful."

There wasn't a dry eye in the church. We were officially united as one in the most magical place on all the earth. After we kissed, our children joined us in the most loving and heartfelt embrace. It was hard to put into words how blessed I felt as this moment. I had never thought I would feel such joy again. Life was perfect.

52

There was something pretty cool about honeymooning with our children. We ate and drank like royalty. We had massage therapists and estheticians come to the villa to provide us with facials and massages. The weather was unseasonably warm, so we were able to utilize the pool and the outdoor hot tub. The only sad thing about our week was that it ended much too quickly. I could have stayed here forever.

The flight back was quiet but peaceful. We all loved our week in Italy. Katharine and I were giddy in love. We spent most of the flight locked up in the cabin, fooling around. The children didn't seem to mind at all; they slept most of the way back anyway.

We had closed on the new apartment right before we left, but we had decided to hang onto the apartments we currently had. Katharine intended to rent hers out to one of the attorneys at the firm who needed a new place to live. The rent was pricey, but he didn't blink an eye at the cost. He worked in the environmental law department, which was proving to be quite lucrative these days. I also intended to keep my apartment as a place for the girls to stay if they didn't want to stay with us. Besides, it was an awesome place, and I didn't want to give it up. I knew it was a great investment.

I got an email the day we landed in Italy that said we had closed on the new apartment. The day after the wedding, we started talking about living arrangements. That was when I surprised her by telling her the closing had been finalized; we were free to move in whenever we wanted. As another surprise to her, I had already moved all of my things, as well as the things she had acquired at my apartment, to our new place. She was thrilled. She knew she wouldn't have time to move when we first got back. After being out of the office for nine days, she thought she would have a lot of work to catch up on. Before we left, however, I called Suzie and asked her to clear Katharine's schedule for the week we were in Italy, so Katharine wasn't totally bombarded with work when she got back. Since the firm was closed for a few days during the holidays, she wouldn't be as overloaded as she initially thought.

She decided to have movers come the following week to pack up and move the rest of her stuff. She had mentioned that she was renting her place furnished, so I took the liberty of having my decorator furnish the new place while we were away. I had suggested using my decorator when we first looked at the place, and she told me she would love having someone else make the decisions. It wasn't something she enjoyed doing. Katharine loved my apartment and said she didn't care if she lived in a cardboard box as long as we lived in the box together. I knew she'd approve of how our new box was decorated.

The limo driver dropped Katharine and Jackson off at her place so she could get organized for the week, and he could get ready to go back to school. The girls wanted to stop by their mother's place to wish her a merry Christmas. I went to my old apartment to see if anything had been left behind, gathered some paperwork I needed, and had my driver take me over to Katharine's. I wasn't planning on spending a night without her. By the time I arrived at her place, it was after 11:00 p.m., and we were exhausted. We crawled under the covers; she thanked me again for our wonderful vacation, wedding and honeymoon; and we passed out.

53

I was excited to see how the decorator had furnished our new place, but I had long hours to put in all week, so we decided to wait until the weekend to go over there and check it out. I knew if we went there now, I'd want to move the rest of my stuff and get organized, and I just didn't have time to do that during the week. Saturday morning, I woke up really early, excited about the move. Ian was sound asleep, so I snuck into the kitchen to make the coffee and start my day. As I was washing out our wine glasses from the night before and waiting for the coffee to finish percolating, I felt hands creep under my shirt onto my bare bottom.

"I thought you were sleeping," I said playfully.

"I got lonely without you, counselor," he said in his deep, husky morning voice. His hands started to roam over my body.

"I didn't go far. I couldn't sleep. I'm excited to see how our new place looks. I'm also a little anxious about moving—I've lived here a long time. On the other hand, I want to be in a place that doesn't hold so many memories of Bryce. I want all new memories with you."

"Well, I think we should start by saying a proper good-bye to this kitchen," he suggested.

He turned me around and lifted me onto the counter. He pulled my shirt off over my head and started sucking on my neck and shoulders, and then he buried himself into my breasts. I wrapped my legs around his waist to pull him closer so I could feel his heat. He continued his assault on my nipples, and I couldn't hold back the sounds that were escaping from my mouth. I used my feet to pull his boxers down, a trick I had gotten pretty good at, and I could feel his arousal hitting the inside of my leg. You'd never know this man was almost fifty years old. He was built like a man in his twenties. And I loved it.

He worked his mouth up to find mine. I reached down and starting stroking him. Like always, he was ready for me. As our kissing deepened, he buried himself inside me, as deep as he could go. I wrapped my legs around his waist, and he grabbed me securely so he could hold me in place and slammed into me as hard as possible. He could always sense how I wanted it—it was a gift. It didn't take long for either one of us to get where we needed to go. God, this was the best way to start a day. But now it was time to check out our new home.

We took our coffee to go and had the driver take us to Greenwich Village, where the new loft was located. It was on the top floor of a magnificent building that had been recently refurbished. When I walked into the front foyer, I was blown away by the spectacular view from the panoramic windows overlooking New York. I knew I'd never tire of the city from this vantage point. I walked around slowly, taking in all of the new furniture and artwork that had been picked out for us. Spaces were left empty for me to add some of the artwork that I had planned to bring with me. The couches were soft and luxurious, upholstered in billowing Italian leather. There were fireplaces in every room, and the marble floors were a sage green that stood out dramatically against the light furniture. The dining set was made of deep mahogany wood, with intricate designs sculpted into the legs and the base. The kitchen was spacious, and I loved the emerald marble countertops. The kitchen cupboards were also mahogany, which made one room seem to flow into the other. When I walked into the master bedroom, I just stood there and smiled. The headboard on the massive bed featured a large, ornate mirror. Ian came from behind me, wrapped his arms around my waist, and kissed my neck.

"Like it?" he asked.

""Whose idea was it to get a mirror?" I asked jokingly.

"That, my dear Katharine, was all my idea. I told Felicia that I thought a mirror would make the room look more spacious," he laughed. Since the master suite could have housed a family of five, the appearance of space was clearly not the issue.

"And did she buy that explanation?" I asked as seriously as I could.

"Probably not, but she's a consummate professional. And I'm paying her—she wouldn't dare question my motives. I would have told her that I love watching myself making love to you in mirrors, but that really wasn't information she needed to know. Should we test it out and see if it was a good idea or not?"

"Lead the way."

For the most part, the move went smoothly. I absolutely loved the new place. It was spacious, beautifully decorated, and had a spectacular view of New York City. Even though I felt a lot of sadness leaving the home I shared with Bryce for so many years, I had no regrets moving forward. That was what was most important to me: believing the decision to marry Ian was the best one for me and for my son. I also thought it was important that we started our life together in a new environment. I think it helped that I didn't sell my apartment. Renting it out seemed to make the transition easier on me emotionally. I called Jack to tell him all about it, and he said he was planning on coming home the following weekend to check it out. The condo had four bedrooms, so all of our children could have their own room. It didn't take long for either of us to make it feel like our home. It was incredible how easy it was to fall into a comfortable routine. It felt like we had been together a lot longer than five months. I was very happy.

54

It was a new year, and I was happier than I could ever have imagined. I had a new home—which I shared with an amazing new wife. Life can be so unexpected sometimes. Katharine and I continued to work hard during the weekdays; that was the kind of people we were. At night, we took turns cooking dinner, cooked together, or went out. It all depended on our mood on any given day. We joked about retiring one day, but we knew it would probably never happen. We loved being in the game. Working hard was important to both of us.

On the weekends, however, we liked to play. We decided that we should make a conscious effort to keep things fresh. Katharine came up with the idea for us to try to do something different every weekend. Sometimes, it was as simple as seeking out a new hot dog vendor. Other times, we would go to a museum or a park. We had thought it would be fun to discover new adventures together, and it was proving to be a blast. If we couldn't figure out anything else to do, we would find a new place to have sex. That was always one of my favorite ideas.

Before we knew it, it was March, and spring was here. New York City really came alive in the spring; it was probably my favorite time of the year. More people roamed the streets. The trees in Central Park started filling in. There were more birds chirping, and the days were longer and brighter. Things were going great until the day I received a frantic call from Sara.

"Dad, it's Mom. She's in the hospital. She tried to kill herself—she overdosed on pills. I need you. Can you please come?" she begged me.

"I'm on my way, sweetheart. Don't worry. Your mother will be all right. She's a strong woman. Where are you?" I asked her.

I called my driver and met Sara in the emergency room at Queens Hospital Center. I was able to get there fairly quickly. I was much more worried about Sara than I was about Monica. In fact, I couldn't remember the last time I'd even given Monica a fleeting thought. Why would she try to kill herself? That didn't make any sense to me at all. She had her pretty boyfriend, she didn't work, and I gave her plenty of money. I couldn't imagine what kind of stress she could possibly have in her life. When I got to the hospital, Sara was sitting by herself, sobbing. She jumped up and ran into my arms when I walked into the room.

"Ok, honey, calm down and breathe. Tell me what happened," I said quietly.

"I guess she saw a picture of you and Katharine at some event, and it sent her over the edge. Em and I never told her you guys got married, and I don't think Mom even knew you were dating anyone. I don't know—maybe we should have told her. But we were afraid she might try to harass you guys or something. We didn't want Katharine to have to deal with any of Mom's crap. Besides, we figured it was none of her business, since she treated you like shit. The caption she saw in the paper said something about how one of the most eligible bachelors in New York was no longer on the market because he had married one of the most beautiful and respected attorneys in the city, blah blah blah, and Mom saw it and went mental! She took a crap ton of pills, and her creepy boy toy found her unconscious on the bedroom floor a couple hours ago. He called nine one one, and then he called me. And here I am. He's with her in the room, so I thought I'd wait for you here. I can't stand being around him. The nurse said they pumped her stomach and are just waiting for her to wake up."

Once Sara got all of that out in what sounded like one giant sentence, she started crying into my chest. I held her for a few minutes, stroking her hair like I had when she was a little girl. No matter how I felt about Monica, I didn't want her to die. Plus, I needed to be there for my girls. There was no way I was going to leave them to deal with this on their own.

"I'd like to see if I could get some more information, sweetheart. Come here and sit down so I can find someone to talk to." I walked her over to a chair, made her sit down, and put my coat around her shoulders—she was shaking uncontrollably. I went up to the nurse's station and explained who I was. She said that she would send the doctor to the waiting room once he was finished examining Ms. Jensen. Dear Lord, it never occurred to me that she had kept my name. I wondered why. So she'd have the last name of her daughters? No, she'd never really cared about them. It was probably just to keep up appearances. She was such a bitch. OK, now was not the time to think like that. I needed to be rational. Now was the time to be compassionate. Sara and Emily needed my support, not my frustration with my ex-wife.

The doctor approached us solemnly and said that Ms. Jensen had indeed overdosed on prescription pills. I briefly wondered what the hell she needed pills for in the first place. Although they had been able to flush some of the toxins out of her stomach, there was still a dangerous amount present in her system. She hadn't been found until several hours after she'd ingested the pills, so quite a bit of damage was still possible. Sara started sobbing again. Even though their relationship was extremely strained, Monica was her mother. I held her close and asked the doctor what the prognosis was. He said that we had to wait for her to wake up and see how her brain was functioning: brain damage was the primary concern at this point. The doctor asked if we had any idea why she had done this—her boyfriend seemed to be completely in the dark.

"She found out that Dad got married again, and she totally and completely freaked," Sara blurted out.

"Well, it's a waiting game for now. We had to put her in a drug-induced coma, and we'll keep her there for the next forty-eight hours to let the swelling in her brain settle down. Once we take her out of that state, we need to hope she wakes up on her own and still has a healthy, functioning brain, " the doctor explained. "We'll let you know if anything changes. Make sure the nurses have all of your contact numbers." And he walked away. We called Emily and told her that she should probably come home. Her first response to the news was "God, she is such a drama queen!" When she heard that brain damage was possible, however, she felt bad and said she'd head back to the city as soon as possible.

I called Katharine and told her what had happened. She was very sympathetic and understood why I needed to be there for the girls. She offered to come, but I told her it was unnecessary. The next couple days were long and ridden with anxiety. The boyfriend was a nice enough guy, but not the brightest bulb in the pack. He had a difficult time understanding the explanations the doctor gave us. After the doctor finished with his daily report of her brain scans and vital statistics, I had to translate everything in terms he could understand. It was a little frustrating, but I wanted to keep things as calm as possible for my daughters. It was obvious that he loved Monica, and I was glad for that. It still pained me to be around him, since it was her infedility with him that led to the demise of our marriage. I'm not sure I'll ever know what motivated her to cheat on me, but it was still difficult. No matter how much I loved Katharine, Monica was the mother of my children. We had a connection that would always be there, regardless of how the marriage ended.

The girls begged me to stay with them, but by day three, Katharine was getting annoyed that I was spending so much time at the hospital. After the way Monica had treated me, she couldn't believe I was putting my life on hold for this woman. She insisted the girls meet her every day for lunch at a restaurant close to the hospital—she wanted to be sure they were eating. She also insisted that they sleep at our place every night. Getting run down or sick wasn't going to help their mother, she insisted. Both girls had contacted their professors and were able to keep up with their studies online. Sara and Emily were both excellent students, so the professors were very understanding. Thank God for modern technology—it made it pretty easy for them to keep up with their work. Things were strained between Katharine and I, but I couldn't help it. Monica was the mother of my children. That was something I couldn't change and didn't want to. Without her, I wouldn't have Sara and Emily, and they were my world.

It wasn't until the seventh day that Monica started to wake up. The four of us were having a glass of wine after dinner and talking about schoolwork when the call came in. The three of us jumped up as soon as we got the news. I called my driver immediately, and we rushed to the hospital. I barely said anything to Katharine as I left, which I didn't realize until I had gotten into the car. I just wanted to know that my ex was OK so we could put this behind us and move on.

When we walked into the room, she looked angry. It was definitely not the look we were expecting. We assumed she'd be groggy and confused, sleepy, or maybe even disorientated. That was not the case at all. The girls were thrilled she was awake, but she completely ignored them.

"How dare you get married again!" she screamed at me.

"Welcome back, Monica. Nice to see you again, too," I said with zero affect.

"Answer me, you jackass! I asked you a question. How dare you get married again?" she repeated.

"My marriage is none of your business. Our daughters have been extremely worried about you, Monica. That was a foolish thing for you to do," I said calmly. I knew my neutral response would piss her off even more, and I didn't care in the least.

"Don't be all reasonable and sensible with me, Ian Jensen. You betrayed me. You knew I'd come back to you. You had no right to marry another woman. You made vows to me. Remember? You promised to love me for better or worse, and you broke those vows. You are a heartless man. I can't even remember why I ever fell in love with you in the first place. But I had planned to forgive you, because we made a vow. You had no right to marry that woman. That wasn't part of the deal we made," she yelled.

"I disagree, Monica. You broke our vows when you jumped in bed with muscle man over there. Infidelity was not part of the deal we made. You destroyed those vows years ago. There isn't a chance in hell that I would ever accept you back into my life again. Why don't you be a good mommy and say hello to your girls? It's been a difficult week for them."

"Go to hell, you bastard. And as for those two, they betrayed me just like you did—they abandoned me and went off to live with you. I washed my hands of both the girls years ago; I had to. You poisoned them with lies and took them away from me. Now look at them. What kinds of daughters choose to live with their father over their mother? I'll tell you. Spoiled ones. They haven't given me a second thought since you all deserted me. Why should I give a rat's ass how they feel now?" she blurted out.

Sara left the room sobbing uncontrollably. Emily stood there frozen for a minute before she said, "We were genuinely concerned for your welfare, Mother, but you have no right to speak to any of us this way. I'd like to say I'm sorry this happened to you, but I'm not. You deserve every bad thing that happens in your life." And with that, Emily left the room, too. I was so proud of what a strong woman she had become. That had to have been very difficult to say, but she had remained poised and direct.

I followed her out and leaned against the wall. I closed my eyes and took a deep breath. At that moment, I couldn't remember how or why I had fallen in love with this hateful woman. She was spiteful and self-ish, and part of me was sorry she hadn't been successful in her suicide attempt. When I opened my eyes, I saw that the girls were hugging. Sara kept saying "she's so horrible," over and over again. My heart was bleeding for them. I walked over to them, put my arms around them both, and told them it was time to go home.

55

I felt like I was participating in an afternoon reality show. My husband was at his ex-wife's beck and call, without a moment's thought of how it made me feel. It was as if I didn't exist. He simply bolted out of here without any consideration. I couldn't believe it. It had been an excruciatingly long week with the three of them at the hospital all of the time. I tried to be as understanding as possible, but it became more difficult every day. Ian was very quiet all week, and I know he was worried for the girls, but our connection was severely strained. We went several days without having sex, which hadn't happened since we'd met. I was confused. Monica hurt him deeply, and he was posting vigil by her side. What the fuck was that about?

They got back to the condo at 11:30 p.m., and I was in bed. When Ian came into the bedroom, I pretended to be asleep. I didn't want to start a fight, I didn't care how Monica was, and I was too hurt to have a conversation with him at this point. He walked to my side of the bed, and I could sense that he was leaning over me. I felt him brush a strand of hair off my face and kiss my forehead. I heard him whisper, "I love you, Katharine," and walk away. Tears slid down my face, but I said nothing and tried to stay as quiet as possible. It took a while, but at some point, I fell asleep.

I got up before the rest of the family the next morning, put on my workout clothes, and snuck out of the house with a change of clothes for work. I didn't have the energy to talk about Monica anymore. I called a friend at the hospital for an update, and she said Monica was recovering nicely. I actually called this friend several times throughout the past week so I didn't have to discuss Monica with Ian or the girls. Oh great, she was going to be fine. I was running on the treadmill and listening to loud music when I saw that Ian was calling me. Oh shit, what was I going to do? I sent the call to voicemail. I needed this workout, and I didn't have the energy to talk to him.

I felt a lot better after running a few miles. I took a hot shower and headed off to work. I thought about calling Ian back, but then I decided that I was still too pissed off; I would deal with it later. I turned my phone off and focused on catching up on the work I had missed thanks to all of the Monica distractions. I needed to think about something else, and work was the only thing that could help me regroup and put things into perspective. At 10:30 a.m., Suzie said Ian was on line one. I couldn't keep avoiding him, so I took the call.

"Morning, Ian," I said quietly and with some hesitation.

"Hey there, counselor. You avoiding me?"

"Not exactly. I just needed to distance myself from all of this Monica drama."

"Are you sure that's all?" he asked.

"I can't talk now. I have a lot of work to catch up on. I got behind the past week spending so much time with the girls. I'll talk to you later." I didn't give him a chance to respond; I hung up the phone and felt like crying. This was crazy. Why was I sad? I should have been pissed off. I should have told him how much he'd hurt me. I should have chastised him for spending so much time by the side of the woman who had ripped their family apart. God, I was such a coward sometimes. I wanted to call him back, but this was a discussion that needed to happen in person. It would have to wait until tonight.

I did feel guilty about running out on the girls, so I sent them a text letting them know that I was here if they needed me, and that I was glad to hear that their mother was going to be OK. Emily thanked me for all of my support and said she was on her way back to school. Sara thanked me for being a better mom than her "bitch-troll horrible excuse for a mom could ever be" and told me that she loved me. What the hell had happened last night?

After I heard from the girls, I set my phone aside. I never thought to turn it off again. When I heard the familiar buzz, I knew who had sent me a message. Ian had sent me a text that simply said, "Dinner?"

"Working late," was my response.

"You're scaring me," he replied.

"Why don't you have dinner with Monica?" was my smartass reply.

"What's that supposed to mean?" he wrote.

"Sometimes you're an ass," was all I could come up with. I regretted it as soon as I sent it, but I couldn't take it back. This whole situation was clearly getting out of hand. Well, I didn't want to deal with it now. I'd face this whole debacle later.

I didn't hear another thing from Ian the rest of the day, and I did stay late at work, even though it wasn't necessary. I didn't want to go home. I was tired and didn't want to talk about it. I realized I hadn't had anything but a cup of coffee and a sports bar to eat all day. I knew I should eat, but I didn't feel hungry. I was worn out, and I felt very alone.

I decided to go see my favorite bartender, Carl, at the bar where Ian and I had met; a gin and tonic and a bite to eat were just what the doctor ordered. It also would kill some time before I had to face my husband and deal with all of this crap. Carl was excited to see me and had my drink ready before I was settled on my barstool. Even though it had been a few weeks since I had been there, he didn't initiate idle conversation. He respected my need for privacy. That was a big reason I enjoyed sitting at his bar. I ordered crab cakes and let my mind wander. I missed Ian. I needed him. I loved him so much. What was I doing? I should be home discussing this whole situation with him. I shouldn't be avoiding him and hiding at the bar like a scorned woman. It wasn't my style. My actions were childish, and very unlike me. I decided to eat the rest of the crab cakes, which were always one of my favorites at this place, and finish my drink. Then I would go home and deal with this like I should have done yesterday. As I was finishing my appetizer, I could feel someone staring at me. I didn't have to look up to know who it was.

"Is this seat taken?" a familiar voice asked me. He was standing behind me, just out of my range of vision but close enough that I could smell his cologne.

"I was saving it for my sexy boyfriend, but I guess you'll do," I said without looking up.

"How sexy is he?" he asked in that deep, husky voice that made my heart race.

"Pretty fucking sexy," I said evenly. "Sadly, he experienced some temporary brain damage and forgot how to use his penis, so I'm coming up with a strategy to figure out how to get it working again," I quipped.

"Forgot how to use his penis, you say? That's disappointing. A beautiful woman like you shouldn't have to go one single day without a well-functioning penis at her disposal. It must have been some serious trauma. I'd love to fill in while he figures out how to get it going again," he offered seductively.

"I don't know—I have pretty high expectations. I require a well-endowed man who can make me climax at least twice during every session."

"I think I'm up for the challenge. Want to check out the goods and see if they're up to your standards?"

I finally looked up from my drink, looked my incredibly sexy husband in the eye, and said, "Yes, I think I would like that very much."

56

I knew this Monica fiasco had been stressful, but I never stopped to think how hard it was on Katharine. It was her remark about taking Monica to dinner that put it all into perspective. She was right. I had neglected her, and that wasn't fair. This whole situation had gotten out of hand. I worried so much about the girls' emotions that I didn't even consider how my wife was dealing with all of this. Katharine was very protective of my daughters and of me, and she knew how badly Monica had hurt all of us. *I was* an ass.

It scared me when I woke up and found that Katharine had left the apartment in the morning without telling me she was leaving for the day. I suspected she was mad, but I had no idea how upset she really was or how much I had hurt her. I don't think she'd ever let one of my calls go to voicemail before. It was a horrible feeling. I hated calling her at work, but I couldn't go all day without speaking to her. When I did call, the conversation left me bereft.

When she blew me off for dinner, I knew I had to do something. I called the office at around 9:00 p.m., and when she didn't answer, I realized where she probably had gone. Familiar surroundings are often very comforting when things aren't going well. If I hadn't found her there, I wasn't sure where else I was going to go. Seeing her sitting alone at the bar brought back a flood of feelings and memories, and I vowed at that moment never to let anyone or anything get between us again. It was too painful.

As I approached her, I was worried she wouldn't talk to me. I was ready for a fight if that's what it took to resolve this. At least a fight would include words: she would be talking to me, and I could hear what was bothering her. It would be progress. A million things went through my mind before I approached her. I didn't know what to say when I walked up to her. I figured asking permission to sit was a good icebreaker. It would give me an idea what kind of mood she was in. I hadn't expected the response she gave me, funny and welcoming. I was so relieved.

We made out the whole ride home, and we promised to talk everything through after she received the pleasure I had promised her. After we finished fooling around, I told her about Monica's outburst and how crushed the girls were. She started to cry. She couldn't believe a mother could speak to her daughters that way. She told me that she would call the girls in the morning to see if they needed to talk about it. I was honest about Monica's reason for the suicide attempt: she had been jealous and angry that I had married again, and she thought her desperate act would be the perfect way to get me back. Monica revolted me, and I told Katharine that. I was very forthcoming with my wife about everything that had transpired. Talking about it with her put the final bit of closure on the situation. I would never let Monica come between us again.

I apologized profusely about neglecting Katharine's feelings. She admitted how hurt she had been, and I finally understood. I had been a total boob. Now that the incident was behind us, it was obvious that none of the Jensen clan was ever going to have anything to do with that horrid woman ever again. She had given me my daughters, which I would always be grateful for. Aside from that, I completely washed my hands of her. She was a hateful woman who had hurt the most important people in my life. From this day forward, I didn't plan to give her another thought. Katharine accepted my heartfelt apology, and we made love again before we went to sleep. God, how I loved this woman.

I made it a point to talk to each of my daughters every day after that. It didn't take long for them to set the incident aside and get back to their routines. They were both excited about the semester coming to an end. I heard that Sara and Jack were hanging out, but I never pried for any information. I figured that if Sara wanted to share anything with me, she would. It was really none of my business. Jack wasn't sharing anything with Katharine, either, so we knew we just had to wait and see. Emily was excited about graduation and her upcoming internship at the law firm, and Martin was still waiting to see where he was going to medical school. It sounded like their relationship was going well. I was happy about that. He was a nice young man who seemed smitten with my daughter. Katharine and I got back into our routine and moved forward.

We rekindled our connection back at Bear Mountain the weekend after the girls went back to school. I reserved the same room, and the staff had it fully equipped without my asking. They kept records of their patrons' preferences, which made us feel very welcome. I ordered a couple's massage, horseback rides through the mountains, and a guided hike tour. It was a magical weekend. All of the crap was truly behind us.

57

I was mortified when Ian told me how that horrid woman had spoken to her daughters. Even though I was not a violent person, I wanted to do vile and aggressive things, to hurt her as much as she had hurt the family I loved so dearly. She must have had some kind of mental problem to attack the girls the way she did. The whole scenario was incomprehensible to me. The more he told me, the more upset I got. I didn't know how anybody could speak in such a hateful manner to another person, especially to her own flesh and blood. It was despicable.

I called Emily first thing the following morning, because I knew she was an early riser and had class at nine. She tended to be more reserved than Sara, so I wasn't sure how much she would open up to me. We had an excellent relationship, but we never spoke as freely about our feelings in the way I was able to speak with Sara. The conversation started out with the usual pleasantries about her ride back to college and her first classes. She had kept up with all of her schoolwork while she hung out at the hospital, so she wasn't behind at all. After a few minutes, I told her that Ian confided in me about the exchange she'd had with her mother.

"I guess her outburst shouldn't have surprised me, Katharine, but it did. She's so mean. Sara ran out of the room crying, which is the only way Sara knows how to deal with things. I'd hoped the whole experience might have changed her for the better, but it did the complete opposite. It made her even more hateful, if that's possible. I can't imagine what we did to make her hate us so much, but she does," Emily said sadly.

"Emily, I don't think she hates you or Sara, because she doesn't even know you. She's too narcissistic to take the time to see what wonderful daughters she created. It sounds like Monica is a very disturbed woman. I'm so proud of the woman you have become, and if she had any sense in her head, she would be, too," I said reassuringly.

"Why can't she be more like you, Katharine? She's never tried to get to know me or support me. She doesn't even know anything about me. She has no idea I'm going to law school in the fall. Isn't that pathetic? I don't even think I've ever had a real conversation with her. And she's my mother, for God's sake. It's not fair." It sounded like Emily was trying very hard not to cry.

"No, it's not fair at all, Emily. Sadly, I don't think Monica is capable of loving anyone besides herself—and to be honest, I don't think she loves herself very much, either. She had the devotion of a wonderful man and two loving daughters and she threw it all away. You and your sister deserve a lot better than that," I said lovingly.

"Thank God we have you in our life now, Katharine. It sucks losing a mom, and she isn't even dead," she said dejectedly.

"I'm sure it does suck. But you do have a mom now. You have me if you'll let me be one for you. Or we could be friends. It's up to you. I want to get to know you so much better. I want to be there for you always. If you let me, I promise to be the best step-mom you could ever imagine, " I told her.

"Let you? You're already the best step-mom Sara and I could ever ask for. We're so happy Dad found you. But, if it's all right with you, I'd like to drop the whole 'step' part of the description. You're the best mom Sara and I could have imagined. We're so grateful for you."

"I'm just as grateful for you, Emily. I always thought I was happy with one child, but I was wrong. Now I have two daughters who I love as much as my own. I feel truly blessed to have both of you girls in my life," I told her.

"We love you just as much. Thank you so much for calling me. I feel bad talking to Dad because of what Mom did to him. It was easier to talk to you about it. I didn't think it would help to talk about what happened, but it really did. It wasn't the same talking to Martin either. He tried to help, but his mom is nice and normal, and it was hard for him to understand how hard this has been. It's been really hard growing up with a mom who didn't care about us. Listen, Katharine, I hate to go, but I have to get to my business law class or I'll be late," she said reasonably.

"Then I'll let you go. But before I do, I need you to promise me something as my daughter, OK?"

"OK, what's that?" she asked eagerly.

"I actually need you to promise me two things. First, I need your promise that you will always be honest with me, no matter how uncomfortable it may make either of us. It's a pact I have with Jackson, and honesty is something I feel very strongly about in my relationships."

"I like that pact, especially since Monica didn't know the definition of honesty. I promise."

"Second, I need you to promise to be my daughter forever, just like I made the promise of forever with your dad," I said.

"You have my promise on both counts," she replied enthusiastically and without any hesitation. And off she went to business law.

The conversation with Sara was very similar, except for the fact that she cried a lot. Emily was much more stoic with her emotions, which would be advantageous when she became an attorney. Sara wore her heart on her sleeve. She was much more demonstrative and cried very easily. Her mother's betrayal had been very hard on her, and I thought some counseling might be very beneficial to her. Sara agreed to my pact of honesty and also to the notion of being my daughter forever. It was a conversation filled with hope and with love. I was so glad I took the time to call these very special young women.

On the drive back from Bear Mountain, I told Ian about the conversations I'd had with his daughters. I needed to reiterate to him how much I loved them and how important a relationship with them was to me. As I was finishing up my story, I felt him slow down and pull to the side of the road.

"Is something wrong?" I asked worriedly.

Ian removed his seat belt so he could turn to face me. "On the contrary, my beautiful wife. Everything is so right. What did I do to deserve a woman like you?" he asked me.

"I could ask you the same thing," I answered.

"Not only have you opened up your heart to me, but you have freely given it to my daughters as well. I'm speechless," he said with tears in his eyes.

"The Jensen clan saved my life, Ian. You know that. When I promised to be your forever, your girls were part of that promise. They needed to know that. They also needed to know how important honesty in a relationship is to me. I can't take the place of their biological mother, but I will spend the rest of my life loving them like a real mother should."

"I don't know what to say. Thank you just doesn't seem like enough," Ian said. It was obvious that he was overwrought with emotion.

I took his face in mine and kissed him lovingly. I loved this man, and I loved his daughters. It was that simple.

"How about you get this car in gear, and I'll figure out a few creative ways you can thank me properly when we get home," I suggested.

"Aye aye, counselor. It would be my pleasure."

Epilogue

There were only two weeks left before all three of our children would be home for the summer. Jack had met with the advertising team over spring break and secured his internship at the company. He had decided to live with us, since the company he was working for was right around the corner from our loft. We had planned to drive to Yale the following weekend to help him move home, but he offered to rent a U-Haul and drive back himself. He was finishing his sophomore year in college. He was definitely an ambitious young man with a bright future.

Emily and Martin got a sublet for the summer near Katharine's law office, which they were very excited about. They thought it would be a good idea to see how they liked living together. The lease started May 15, which gave them three months of playing house before Emily went off to law school. Martin got a full-time job at a restaurant near the apartment as well. Waiters and waitresses tend to make good money in New York City, and he needed to make as much as possible to help pay for school. He had been accepted into medical school at NYU and was excited to start the program in the fall.

Sara still wasn't sure what she was going to do when the semester ended. She was always waiting until the last minute to make decisions. We had a room for her at our new place, and my other apartment was also available for her to use if she wanted. I hadn't been to my old apartment for about two months, so I needed to have my cleaning crew go over and give it a deep clean in case she decided to live there. I couldn't imagine that it had gotten too dirty, but I wanted it ready either way. I wasn't worried that she didn't have a definitive plan. She was always re-sourceful and would figure something out at the last minute. I loved her spontaneity.

Katharine had sent me a message earlier in the day saying that she wanted to go to Pane Vino for dinner. She was craving my brother's la-sagna. I told her I could meet her at about seven o'clock. I needed to go back to the old apartment first and get some documents out of my safe. I hadn't been back there for several weeks. I loved the place and sometimes missed living there, but I loved my new home with Katharine much more. Buying the new place together had meant a lot to the both of us.

I was checking an e-mail on my phone as I walked into the apart-ment. I had just responded to one of the messages when I looked up and was mortified by what I'd walked in on.

"What the fuck are you doing?" I blurted out.